I0642565

2022

Writing from Inlandia

An Inlandia Institute Publication

Riverside, California
2023

Executive Director: Cati Porter
Publications Coordinator & editor: Maria Fernanda Vidaurrazaga
Publications Assistant: Caitlyn Johnson
Book layout & design: Mark Givens

Printed and bound in the United States
Distributed by Ingram

Published by Inlandia Institute
Riverside, California
www.InlandiaInstitute.org
First Edition

2022 Inlandia Creative Writing Workshop Leaders

Richard Allen May III

Allyson Jeffredo

James Ducat

Victoria Waddle

Jo Scott-Coe

Romaine Washington

Renee Gurley

Jose Chavez

Carlos E. Cortés

Lydia Theon Ware i

John Brantingham

Jerry Mathes

Stephanie Barbé Hammer

Alaina Bixon

Lisa Henry

James Coats

Carlee Franklin

Cait Johnson

Frances J. Vásquez

Mae Wagner

Wil Clarke

Rose Y. Monge

This event is supported in part by an award from the National Endowment for the Arts. To find out more about how National Endowment for the Arts grants impact individuals and communities, visit www.arts.gov.

This activity is also supported in part by the California Arts Council, a state agency. Learn more at www.arts.ca.gov.

Contents

Autumnal Tiki Lounge

BY JANET LAKO ALEXANDER

Sit back, relax
Enjoy a vibrant lifestyle
Here at the retirement village

…just like the skeleton couple
on my neighbor's porch.
They sit straight-backed,
white bones on black wrought iron chairs.
Four little tiki warriors,
menehune with surfboards,
stand guard at their feet.

The skeletal gent and his bony wife
both rock real banana-leaf skirts.
A lei of shiny foliage
adorns his frame. More leaves
encircle his head and wrists.
The missus dazzles—her tropical
orange, lime, and blue flowers
crown her auburn-wigged skull
and drape around her coconut shell bra.

Skele-Tom nurses a pineapple
cocktail, while their little dog,
Calaca Chihuahua,
stands on the round table
ready to bark at passersby
or the twittering sparrows

under drooping hawthorn,
fig and eucalyptus trees.

Skeletrina gazes
into the crystal ball
grasped in her rootlike fingers.
Who knows what future she sees
as the crows caw
and the too-warm sun lowers
in the October sky?

Blues for Stevie Ray

After Langston Hughes

BY JANET LAKO ALEXANDER

Won't you ease my heart
with some slow Texas blues?
Won't you ease my heart
with the soul of those blues?
No one plays them better
than Stevie Ray used to do.

He leaned over his guitar,
riverboat hat, flash of rings.
He leaned over his guitar,
his large hands bent the strings.
He moaned a low moan
guitar thrummed, dragonfly's wings.

Brown-eyed voodoo child
made cool lightning fly,
that brown-eyed voodoo child
with his sweet soul's cry,
a heart big and lonesome
as a blue Texas sky.

He laid down that guitar
and said, *I'll see you soon.*
He laid down his guitar,
and reached up for the moon.
Shined it like a silver concho
till the whole night rang in tune.

Marigolds

BY JANET LAKO ALEXANDER

orange and yellow
their ruffled petals
burst with joy

their dark, spicy smell
mingles with the scents
of fruit and candles
offerings on the altar

glowing marigolds
small, fiery suns
that light the way
for ancestors to return

Cempasúchiles

POR JANET LAKO ALEXANDER

anaranjados y amarillos
sus pétalos como rizitos
estallan de alegría

su olor oscuro y especiado
se mezcla con los olores
de las frutas y las velas
ofrendas en el altar

cempasúchiles brillantes
pequeños soles de fuego
que alumbran el camino
para que los ancestros regresen

If I Could I Would

The latest school shooting in Texas has shocked and also angered many people.

BY MARGIT ANDERSSON

Small children are now being massacred in the name of the Second Amendment. So if I could, I would change people's mind about that.

As I see it, the Second Amendment isn't Holy Scripture. It is man made, reflecting a time when the threat of tyranny from abroad was a concern. It wasn't created to allow for a sort of hobby for some to be able to kill lots of people at one time because it was so easy. So if I could, I would make the True Believers consider that.

To bring up mental health or mental illness issues in connection with the shootings is to put the cart before the horse, so to speak. It obfuscates the real problem which is staring in everyone's face, namely the too easy access to guns for everyone, sane or not. To have a crystal ball and somehow foresee who is mentally ill enough to plan and carry out mass murder is impossible. And mere suspicion of such plans is even more impossible as a tool for prevention. People can't be committed or incarcerated because of a mere suspicion in this country.

The "solutions" suggested by some politicians are so absurd or impractical that no one should take them seriously.

To regulate gun ownership doesn't stop crime, or stop the so called Bad guys from doing bad things. People would still become murder victims, one way or another. But it would stop the current insanity of mass murder where children are sacrificed on someone's altar they call the Second Amendment.

The easy access to all types of guns has reached a craziness level that possibly one day will reach a tipping point.

If I could, I would make the people who are opposed to any kind of gun control realize that as it is, NO one is safe and that making it difficult to obtain a gun would not be the end of the world.

October

by Margit Andersson

October is a melancholy month because I mostly associate that month with death.

My nephew, Dan, that young man 21 years of age, died in an accident. The devastation of the family and the grief was overwhelming, bottomless. At the funeral, the church was full of friends, neighbors, family. I remember Anna, their old neighbor, clad in all black and how she curtsied deeply in respect before the coffin as she placed a flower on the lid.

Another October, October 2, was the day of my mother's funeral and interment. And how it snowed that day, big wet snowflakes slowly falling on the grass. Visible across the fields was the cemetery where the family grave was located. I wanted to attend and was there as the coffin was being lowered into the ground. I let a note written by a grandchild drift down to the coffin. Her namesake, Hanna, 8 years old, wanted her grandmother to have it with her that way.

My mother's old cat, Orvar, her companion during her last years, knew or sensed what had happened. How could he not. But again the snowfall, on the wet ground, the cat sat staring across the fields toward the graveyard the whole time it took for the coffin to be brought there and to be lowered into the ground and then covered.

Everything was still there, the house, the kitchen, the coffee cups and the pots and pans, the trees, the grass, the forest. But the heart of that whole existence, that environment, was gone, it had stopped beating. Nothing was the same, and everything became a memory.

Accidental Angel

by Don Bennet

It was a warm spring day. I called my wife to tell her that I would be a little late coming home. I had to finish a document that needed to be filed at the courthouse in the morning. I left the office about 6:30 and drove home. When I got home, my wife had been busy all day, and was ready to get out of the house. We decided to go out for dinner. After dinner, on our way home, we passed a bar in town that was frequented by locals. As we drove by, we noticed to our left a figure in the drainage ditch. I stopped the car and approached the figure, which turned out to be a woman who was probably in her 50s. She appeared to be very inebriated and her pants were wet. I grabbed her by the arm and pulled her up.

As she spoke, her speech was a little slurred as she said to me, "Bless you! You are an angel!" Meanwhile, my wife had found some newspaper in the back of the car, and she spread it out on the front passenger seat to protect the upholstery. Once I got the woman situated in the car, we asked her where she lived.

She indicated the route by pointing every time we came to an intersection.

We drove approximately two miles before we reached the street where she said she lived. I pulled into the driveway of a house that had a garage behind the house, down the driveway. I got her out of the car and walked her up to the back door of the house.

I could see that the door opened into a kitchen. Just as she opened the door, a large young man in his 20s approached from a different room. The woman entered and disappeared into the house. He watched her walk by and then turned back to me. The young man looked at me and scoffed, "You shouldn't have bothered. You should have left her there." I didn't answer him, but just turned around and went back to the car. Apparently this wasn't the first time that she had returned home drunk.

As we drove home, I said to my wife, "I hope we don't get stopped on the way home. This car reeks so bad that if we were stopped, a policeman would think *we* had been drinking!" It would be hard to explain why our car smelled like 80- or 90-proof. After we got home, we left the windows of the car down in order to air it out. Such are the woes of an accidental angel.

Old Door Knob

by Don Bennet

This is a work of pure fiction. None of the names or places contained herein are real. They are merely the musings of an old mind, decrepit though it may be. The mention of a guy named Marvin is completely coincidental to anybody I might know by that same name, although I do know a guy named Marvin who's really handy.

The giant, old house was built before 1900. It was a boarding house in the mining town of Goldfield, Nevada. The state was putting a highway near where the house stood, so it either had to be moved or demolished. A house mover named Mr. Roberts and his crew undertook the job of moving it to Las Vegas, some 194 miles away. Mr. Roberts was a hunchback because in a previous house move, a house had fallen on him. This time, they cut the house into three parts. They loaded it up and off they went, not without some degree of difficulty.

There were several things connected to the house, including a front door which had an ancient door knob on it. The house was taken over and lived in by a very old lady who was quite short. She was about as tall as a yardstick. Many of the local children liked her and would come over to visit from time to time. The day before Halloween, during one of the visits by the children, the door knob fell off. The woman really did not know what to do, but with the help of her neighbors, she called Marvin's Fix It Shop for help. Marvin was booked already on Halloween, but he had time available the day after that.

On Halloween, the door knob was still missing, so the old lady put a little table with a big bowl out on the front porch. There was a note in front of the bowl that said, "Take one." Inside the bowl she put little boxes of raisins. The morning after Halloween, the woman went to retrieve her table and the bowl, and she was surprised to see that the bowl was still full. There was a note written in a child's hand that said, "No, thank you!"

That morning, when Marvin arrived, she noticed that his van had a sign on it with his name and the phrase, "No job is too small for a little helping hand." He reattached the door knob, and as he was leaving, he said to her, "I'm going to leave you a little something that may help with other small issues you have. It always helps me. In fact, a friend told me that you can use it for arthritis. I use it on my knees, and it works like a charm. I just don't use it on Sundays, because I don't want to go to church smelling like a tractor." He reached into his pocket, took out a can of WD-40, and handed it to her.

What's something you've done that you never thought you would do?

by Karen Bradford

Life is not measured by the number of breaths we take,
but by the moments that take our breath away.

My life is a collection of things that I never thought I'd do: When God was handing out adventure genes, I must have gotten in line twice, and if reincarnation is true, I must always have been born under the sign of Sagittarius, the traveler of the universe.

I've traveled throughout the world numerous times and often by myself. I went to Scandinavia to see where my grandparents came from, and I just kept expanding my trip from there, thinking I might never get to that area again ... and that's how I ended up in Moscow when I started out for Southern Sweden!

It was right after the Soviet Union had broken up, and even my Russian friend said it was not safe to travel alone, so I joined a very small tour group in Helsinki. Our young Finnish tour guide's English was perfect, except that he pronounced v's as w's. As we first gathered to get on the bus for St. Petersburg, he cautioned that the former Soviets under communism had absolutely no idea of what "customer service" meant, so perhaps instead of thinking of the next week as a "waycation," we should instead think of it as an "adwenture."

Most of my life has been an adwenture, and I like it like that: "Live! Otherwise, ya got nuthin' to talk about in the locker room!"

In college, I studied in East Africa where I camped my way through Kenya and Tanzania; watched the sunsets glow off the snows of Kilimanjaro; played Frisbee with Maasai warriors on the Serengeti Plains; slept on the floor of a bar overlooking Ngorongoro Crater when there truly was "no room at the inn" and was treated to a glorious sunrise, the lakes inside the crater looking like globules of mercury from the reflected dawn; camped with lions roaring outside of my tent; and came face to face with a mother elephant and her baby, sure I would die the next moment, squished under her gigantic foot. I danced in the arms of my shy, young Kikuyu professor on the terrace of a hotel above the Indian Ocean as the waves crashed below us in the lushly warm and softly humid tropical night. (He later said I'd make a very good second wife.)

I rebuilt the engine of my own sportscar, a 1960 MGA; hiked to the top of Mt. Whitney, highest point in the continental United States; I've been robbed at gunpoint — twice — and still kept my cool. I've been shaken down by Maoist insurgents in Nepal as their fundraiser; felt in touch with the cosmic universe standing at the great citadel rock at Machu Picchu; and stood at the Tibet-side base camp of Mount Everest — twice — and decided I would never be in a church or temple more holy than what I felt looking up from right there.

I've traveled to places most people have never heard of — the Tiger's Nest Monastery in Bhutan (a country whose major city is notable by being the only world capitol without a traffic light, it instead has a "dancing policeman"), the Guge Kingdom in far western Tibet — and I pony-trekked around its very sacred Mount Kailash, sleeping in monasteries at night.

I've black-water rafted through caves radiating blue with glow-worms in New Zealand. I've galloped horses along the beach in Kenya; through fragrant eucalyptus forests in Queensland, Australia; amidst spiky lava fields in Iceland, and between pre-Colombian temples in Peru after dodging trucks and cars as we bolted across the Pan-American Highway to get there. I learned to jump horses when I was in my fifties, but as one of my friends incredulously asked, "*Over* fences? Not along the *side* of fences?"

My friends have learned better than to double-dog dare me because my axioms are: "Leap out of the rut!" and "I'll try anything once, so long as it doesn't hurt *too* badly."

My next adwenture? Rappelling off the top of an 11-story office building in downtown Riverside on May 21 to raise money for a Habitat for Humanity veterans housing project in Jurupa Valley. I'm selling sponsorships to come watch me: I'll be the one wearing a Spandex leopard costume, my face painted with spots and leopard ears zip-tied to my helmet!

Write about your biggest learning challenges in school (academic or social).

How did you cope?

BY KAREN BRADFORD

As I sat on the tall swivel chair at the breakfast bar overlooking our small kitchen, I heard my mother's Chevy Impala pulling up the long driveway between our house and the neighbor's block wall. I was tired, just home from the first day of my senior year in high school. A sluggish sense of exhaustion, finality and evitability echoed ahead of her car like a tidal wave, and I instantly understood my father was dead.

In the mid-'60s, there was no word yet for Alzheimer's. He had started forgetting things, but what intellectual person doesn't after learning so very much? He was a geologist and had told me about how the world formed, but the day when he was driving and turned our car into oncoming traffic, my mother and I knew everything in our lives had forever changed.

I cannot remember a single moment of his funeral, but I remember the agonizing moments of trying to fit back in school after I returned a week later. When one of my classmates mimicked her "senile granny," I wanted to twist and mash Adrienne's face into the vents of her gym locker until it oozed pulp from the other side as I shouted, "You're talking about my father!" I raged silently, of course.

I was editor of the school newspaper, and our advisor let me stay in his classroom every day for lunch, ostensibly to continue working, in reality to hide from having to try to act like a normal, chatty teenager instead of the heartbroken and lonely child that I was.

I was the only one of four children left at home, and I now realize my mother must have been drinking herself into numbness at her unexpected widowhood at age 60, and I didn't want to go home. I must have looked unbearably pathetic at the end of each day as I lingered in my last English class, like some current-day Oliver Twist, my eyes asking my teacher: "Please, sir, may I have some more, please?"

More of your time, more of your attention, more of anything to help me put off going home?

How the loss of a parent changed your perspective of life

BY KAREN BRADFORD

I've been friends with Alice for more than 50 years: since we were in high school. When her father died last year, she said something so incredibly stupid that I wanted to slap her and shout, "You can't be serious! Just listen to yourself!"

She told me that I was "lucky" not to have 50 years of my father in my life being suddenly ripped away, as hers was then, leaving a fountain of pain spewing like a sheared-off fire hydrant. "You selfish bitch" was what my heart cried, but, of course, my brain checked me from saying that to my beloved friend.

I never had the chance to build 50 years of memories to sustain me through pain that has continued while hers had just started. My father had started losing his mind to Alzheimer's, which no one yet understood in the mid-1960s when I was entering my teen years.

Instead of having a father who would caution me about wild boys with "Roman hands and Russian blood" (roaming hands and rushing blood, that is, raging hormones!) or advise future dates about bringing me home on time, instead my mother sent me to find my father when he wandered off down the street, and I desperately pleaded with him to come with me — praying he recognized me — praying none of my friends saw me trying to drag home my large Swedish father. Once, the police department had to help us search for him.

Alice never went through that.

My father had been a geologist. When I was little, we were the only ones in the family who woke up early on weekends, so as he made coffee, he plopped me on the kitchen counter and talked about rocks: Igneous! Metamorphic! Sedimentary! On vacations, we collected rocks and sands, and he pointed at geographic features, explaining why they looked the way they did and the erosive forces of nature.

Later in life, when I studied plate tectonics in the Rift Valley of East Africa and traveled to Mount Everest — twice! — as I got closer and closer to it, already understanding the folded and contorted Himalayas, I sent my thoughts out into the universe: "Daddy! I was the one who paid attention! Of your four children, *I'm* the one who's most like you!"

And Alice feels sorry for herself …

But me, I never got to say: "Daddy, teach me everything you know … Daddy, I'm on the Dean's List! *Again!* … Daddy, he's the one I want to marry … Daddy, you're going to be a grandfather!"

Alice got to have all of those … and more.

It was my two big brothers who did their best to help me grow up: teaching me to drive, teaching me to repair my car and giving a surly eye to boys who came calling. I'm sure, however, I never would have married my first husband if my daddy had been alive: My fiancé was older, and he provided the attention I was looking for in my life.

Nowadays, with my parents' generation all gone, I long to be able to ask, "Daddy, what do you think?" I don't feel nearly smart enough, wise enough, and that is what I missed by not having the opportunity of a father's guidance throughout my life.

Alice did.

Taco and Pettie, the Chihuahua Mighty Dogs

AKA Taco's Memoir

BY MARY BRIGGS

I am big, I am mighty, I am Taco, the Chihuahua dog! Big and brave, tall and mighty! I devour all who stand in my way! I flounce along, Oops, I mean I march along on my big huge feet! Brave and strong, mean, mighty, I guard the weak! I guard the frail and old!

What's that I see, a horse, Naw!...a giant evil thing. Let me at him!! I'll protect you little Pettie. Not to worry. 1,000 lbs. you say he weighs six feet tall! Nothing just a drop of piss in the bucket!

I am big! I am strong! I am Taco, the Chihuahua, Hua, Hua, Hua, dog! Giant, brave of heart, I protect! I protect all, the small, the weak, the frail!

What is this, a snail!...in a shell? Why do you hide little brother? Be not afraid, no more! Taco, brave and mighty dog is here. I'll devour all!

Pettie, my dear brother! Get up and run. Let's climb that hill. Oh! Oh! Two giant dogs! Let's go trash them! I'll take one, you take the other! When I finish with mine, I'll go help you. Only should you need help, of course. You can handle it Bro, Go! Go! Go! Petti, Go! Get that big brown giant dog!

And when we're done with thrashing them, we'll dance a jig and shout and sing a bawdy song. A toast, champagne, to celebrate our victory! Nawww, give me a beer instead. And don't forget my steak, our steak, that is!

Come along! Pettie Dear. Let's go find a new adventure! For I am! Or rather we are! Big and mighty, brave and mean Chihuahua giant dogs!!!

I Am a Child of the Sun

by Mary Briggs

Absorbing the nectar of the Gods
My backyard hills and field, of my valley home
Waking up, rushing outdoors
Planning just 15 minutes of Vitamin D
Ends 2 hours later
With an aching back,
Aching arms and fingers stiff
And a happy heart
Pulling weeds on hands and knees
Eating Dandelion leaves and flowers
Climbing hills on hands and knees
Hoeing, raking, pruning trees
Finally weary, stumbling
Collapsing on a white plastic patio chair
Now, sitting on my patio chair
Watching, listening
Feeling the warmth of the sun
The cool of the breeze
Watching a squadron of bees
Like Helicopters hovering
Around a flowering bush
Nearby a solitary hummingbird
Candy apple green, red chested
Sipping nectar
From a yellow flower of an Aloe Vera plant
Soon my pets come to visit me
How's my little precious lizard, I coo

As he rushes by, stops a foot away
Listens, turns his head
I keep on cooing
He stops, turns and looks at me
Makes eye contact
Then skitters off
I'm envious, he can do push ups, I can't
And rabbit runs across the hill
Disappears, where did he go
My eyes search the hill, nothing
I spot a lone ground scratching bird
Pecking the ground for food
Hop scratch, hop scratch
Finds a speck of food
Swallows it
I hear different bird calls
I listen, search the trees
Listen more
I rest my back, on my patio chair
Absorb the Sun, feel the breeze
Listen to the birds, watch the bees
The rabbits, the squirrels
My eyes search for the little lizard
Watching, listening to all that live
In my little bit of Paradise

The Shelves Are Empty Now

BY MARY BRIGGS

The shelves are empty now
Stripped clean upon Covid-19 shutdown
Panic struck, fear prevailed
Survival mode took root

They came in droves
Grabbed, pushed, shoved, fought
Over water and toilet paper

First aid supplies, gone
Food in short supply
Out of supermarkets
Out of Walmart, Costco and Sam's Club
Overflowing shopping carts
Unloaded onto cars, SUV's and trucks
Trunks filled to capacity

The streets are nearly empty now
Schools closed and silent
No more children walking home
No more cars chauffeuring them home
Home is now the classroom
Laptop the teacher

Libraries closed their doors
Lonely books gather dust
No one to hold them and caress them anymore

Restaurants have shut their doors

No lights to beacon you
No aroma to draw you in
Empty booths, rotting food
Some doors will forever close

Hardware stores are filled with project seekers
Lines are long and patient
People buying plants and gravel
And multi wooden projects

The brave who venture out
Wear masks and rubber gloves
Carry hand sanitizers
Fearfully keep six feet apart
Avoid their neighbors
Home is refuge now
More than ever
During Coronavirus, Covid-19

Where Did My Bambi Go

BY MARY BRIGGS

So gentle a nature
So calm and peaceful
He seemed
Never got angry
Never said an unkind word
Pacifist always
Unresponsive to all offense
YET!!!
I touched
What?   When?   How?
A rage I could not control
He could not control
What button did I touch?
What did I say or do
To create the Frankenstein in him?

I sit frighten to the core
Afraid to say or do
How do I regain my gentle giant?
How do I change Frankenstein back to Bambi?
How do I get my Bambi back?

I Am Pandemic

BY STEPHANIE A. BRUCE

I invaded like a thief in the night. Bringing my army of darkness to cover your world with fear and uncertainty. First I brought a fear that few of you had ever seen. I caused you to lay blame where it didn't belong. I created uncertainty about the continuation of life on your world.

I stole the lives of your older people, your sick. Even though I didn't steal the lives of the young as much, I stole their normalcy and happiness. I caused the children depression that some are not getting over to this day.

As I marched forward across your world I stole, I also stole the music, the coming together in worship and faith around the world was gone, disappeared. Many lost their livelihoods.

I STOPPED TIME.

Some of you fought me with science, intelligence and common sense. Some of you didn't believe I was real, even though you witnessed my wrath.

I caused division. That is what I came here to do. I watched as friends and family were put on opposite sides of what you were told to do. Opposite sides in their belief of me. Political division, that was my greatest accomplishment.

Even though I have departed from your world for now…I WATCH. I wait for the slightest opening with which to grab a hold of your world again. Never doubt me. Be aware I am still here. Choose wisely and be cautious.

Fight my aftermath with LOVE. For that is what will keep me away. Your love for one another, your caring for your fellow human beings.

From the Uni Van

BY GEORGETTE GEPPERT BUCKLEY

A plethora of unis
sporting uniform unitards
roll out

Riding universal unicycles
Into figure eights
while balancing parasols

Chanting Uni-uni-UNI
protected by unicorns
pacing the park's perimeters

To the ukulele troupe's
undying staccato strums
and spontaneous bongo drums

The unencumbered giggles
of delighted children
prancing on the grass

Their parents
clapping to the beat
and tapping their feet

Until the sun starts to set
in the deluge
they get wet

Children and parentals
alight the unicorns
flying across the universe

Sight

BY GEORGETTE GEPPERT BUCKLEY

Waiting for eyelids to heal
blurring vision
dropping lubricant

Repeating icing
elevating
tea bagging

Ointment seeping
double visioning
vision doubling

Drop missing eye
trying again
lubricating

Bruising reddening
yellowing
bluing

Head aching bending
light sensitive
huge sunglasses and hat shading

Dropping second
antibiotic anointing
stopping bending

Bulging eyelid
smarting
resting?

Toiling
waiting
to see

Sounds

by Georgette Geppert Buckley

Can you:
look at a spiraling rhythmical painting and hear music?
stand in a forest and communicate with whistle language?
make musical instruments by hand from kelp or wood?
see colors when you close your eyes?

Does:
a specific scent or sound remind you of an event?
the black text while reading turn a different color?
a certain song remind you of a past event?

Do you hum spontaneously?
Can you experience another form of synesthesia or super power?
Let me hear your thoughts.
We are among you.

Some of these ponderings stem from experiencing the exhibit,
Sounds, at El Camino College Gallery, curated by Michael L.
Miller, Director.

Made American

BY LESSLIE ALVAREZ BURHANS

I'm not sure when I started hiding. If I were to set a day, it would be the day my foot stepped over an imaginary line. A line created to end a two-year war, and the occupation of a country. A line that resulted in the loss of California, New Mexico, Nevada, Utah, Arizona, Colorado, parts of Wyoming, Oklahoma and Kansas, those territories were with a flick of a pen taken and made American. During a visit to Colorado to stay with a friend who I met in kindergarten in Brooklyn, NY, she was showing me the sights and pointing out mountain ranges. She mentioned how surprised she was at the number of Mexicans in Colorado. Yes, I suppose it is surprising that 170 years after our land was taken, we had the audacity to remain there. My chest tightened but I remained silent.

I don't remember hiding in Mexico, granted I only have a handful of memories, I was four when I was taken away and made American. I was my parents' second daughter and never the favorite, my skin was the color of café con leche, my hair black wild and curly, the opposite of my older and fairer sister. No one preferred me, not my mother who called my sister her best friend, nor my father who barely knew me having left right after my birth looking for work up north, not even my grandmother who took care of me while my mother worked was impartial. She nicknamed me bruja for my cloud of hair that refused to be tamed.

I learned my first lesson on hiding, and the importance of fading into the background on an evening walk with my mother and older sister across a patchy well-worn dirt path. I didn't recognize the people who were whispering and walking with us, I didn't know why we were all so somber or why my mother had gathered all our clothes into two small homemade bags with Strawbery

Shortcake emblazoned on them. My mother held my hand a little too tightly, but I didn't complain. Suddenly, I tripped, fell, scraped my knee, the crickets cried out, my mom gasped and gripped me tighter, but I didn't cry out. Later my mother would tell the tale of what a good girl I was for being so quiet and holding in my pain while crossing the border, the imaginary line that delineated where hope could grow like wildflowers. As an adult I wondered how I knew the seriousness of our evening walk. Was it visceral? Was it how a cat knows to hide in the far reaches of under a bed? Perhaps it was something learned or passed down to me like my cleft chin and brown eyes.

From that walk we took a plane to NYC where I grew up in Sunset Park Brooklyn. Us kids were not allowed outside. My father perceived danger standing in every corner holding brown paper bags. The boys stood by the corner bodega being loud, loud with their baggy pants and wife-beaters, loud with their laughs and their greetings towards me of "Hey mami, why don't you say hello!", loud with their hip-hop music from their boomboxes, hanging out until it was too late to go to school the next day. We were prohibited from making friends with anyone on our block and on hot summer days the most we were allowed to do was sit on our stoop and watch other kids play stickball and run through open fire hydrants. I passed my time reading and watching TV. They were my only friends and teachers. The TV shows that raised me from Scooby Doo to Full House all had one thing in common, beloved white girls as their protagonists. Even the telenovelas my mother hurried to watch at 7pm every evening had a fair-skinned woman as the love interest and heroine. The only brown people I saw on TV were portrayed as gang bangers, East L.A. cholos, maids or gardeners. When I did see a fellow brown girl on TV like Jessica Alba, she would state she was not Mexican, she was American. Her shame was so heavy that I felt its weight from across the country in my bedroom in Sunset Park Brooklyn. I carried it in my pocket and pulled it out, everytime people asked "where I was from" or noted how exotic I looked.

Pop culture didn't show Mexican-Americans like the Chemist, Luis Miramontes who co-invented the contraceptive pill, or Ellen Ochoa an astronaut and former Director of the Johnson Space Center. Nor did I see a Lesslie with two s's, Chief Financial Officer, MBA, whose love for Led Zeppelin was only matched by her love for Juan Gabriel. The Mexican people I encountered said I wasn't really Mexican anymore, I had been in the States for too long, TV told me daily that I wasn't American either because I was missing nine numbers. It seemed everyone knew exactly what I wasn't except me. I was neither American or Mexican, I was hovering lost between the two worlds, it seemed to me that the line I crossed many years before had been a wormhole that took me into limbo.

My parents spoke Spanish to us kids, even taught me to read in Spanish, but they were never shy about their preferences, white good, brown bad. The fact that my father was the color of cinnamon didn't matter. He spoke in reverence of my mother's light skin, how she turned pink in the sun, and had eyes the color of honey. Years before 23andme my father cataloged my mother's DNA, hypothesizing about European ancestry, certain that she was one of the lucky ones. As a child, you don't realize you are listening to propaganda, subliminal messages, you just learn and encode.

At the age of 35 holding an MBA a step away from the C-suite, living in the house of my Pinterest dreams, a family of my own, and a Citizen, I realized I was still hiding. If my parents were fucked up because they had been poor, undocumented, uneducated, and barely scraping by, then I should have been healed. I should have been in rapture; happiness should drip off me like the jewels I wore. Why then did I continue to hide behind that heavy cloak of fear and shame I acquired when crossing the border? Digging deep, letting my ego lay bare its truth, I heard it whisper "I don't hide because I am unwanted, I feel unwanted because I am not white." I heard the truth, saw it wrapped around my heart like a parasite, keeping it in constant tightness and anxiety. My therapist suggested researching my history, perhaps doing an actual DNA test.

During my historical exploration I found the battle that created the invisible line that I crossed those many years ago.

The line was decided upon 140 years before in a battle lost in the center of Mexico City. The Palace of Chapultepec a Nahuatl word meaning "hill of the grasshopper", is a fortress that stands on a hill sacred to the Aztecs. The Palace housed the national military school young trainees aged 10 years old to 20. 7,000 troops from the north attacked 800 soldiers protecting the fortress. The slaughter was swift and merciless. The story goes, that Juan Escutia a young trainee, came to the realization that the battle was lost, and rather than surrender to the enemy, he wrapped himself in his country's flag and jumped 200 feet from the Palace's walls, refusing for the flag and himself to be captured by the invaders.

After reading this tale all I wanted was to emulate Escutia, I wanted to jump before the enemy finished their capture so I wrapped myself in the Mexican flag and jumped. No more hiding. Preferring to die, lose friends, lose opportunities, than to let the invaders take me alive. The invaders that lived inside of me. I spoke my truths to all who I encountered: "I am proudly Mexican, that comment is racist, we are oppressed, no we don't all have accents, no we don't all know each other, fuck *American Dirt* that shitty book", and to my parents; "I am brown, and I am beautiful, and so are you"

What A Poem Should Do

A Thought Poem

by Alben Chamberlain

A poem should tell a story
that everyone can understand.
What good is a set of beautiful lines that cannot
be understood by 90% of the people in the land?

A poem should, therefore, have a
beginning, middle, and an end.
It doesn't matter that, many of the literary
rules and conventions, you must bend.

There ought to be a person telling the story,
with a clear tone and a point-of-view.
Without a memorable character or voice,
a poem is as useful as a worn-out shoe.

A poem ought to aspire to making the reader
think about the world or society all around.
Too many writers of poems merely endeavor
to make us fall in love with a cadence or sound.

The story must rouse emotions
in the writer and the reader too.
Otherwise, it's just an exercise in word
structure—fit only for a literary review.

A poem should reflect the culture of
the writer and their place and time.

Still, a poem should aspire to cast light on
the human condition by accident or design.

A poem should make people think, laugh,
experience wonder, get angry, or cry.
I would hope to write a poem that
would do all five of these before I die.

Love Expressed By Busy Hands

A Praise Poem

by Alben Chamberlain

My wife has a way of expressing
love using her hands and her heart.
She perfected it even during the time
when the pandemic kept friends apart.

She looked forward to retirement so she
could get together with friends and knit.
Alas, those plans seemed to be dashed
when the vile COVID pandemic hit.

When it seemed that driving to a knit shop
or cafe to knit and kibitz seemed doomed,
technology came to the rescue allowing
old friends to get together via Zoom.

I used to laugh as she knit and talked
to a laptop computer propped up on books.
It became a weekly gathering of fellow knitters
with digital faces of her friends everywhere she looked.

The technology brought kindred spirits together,
yet love is what they gathered to share.
They would talk about projects and patterns,
family members, and troubles they had to bear.

It wasn't the same as gathering together in person
to spend a morning knitting and talking story.

Still, it was a break from looking at the walls
closing in and a life in quarantine that was boring.

Through knitting, she's made friends
with ladies from all around this vast land.
Many are snowbirds who come to Southern
California when the cold gets out of hand.

They surprise each other on birthdays,
with gifts, FaceTime calls, and communal meals.
They know they're not getting younger,
as passing time, their days and energy steals.

My wife has knitted baby blankets for neighbors,
and new mothers to whom she's not related.
Expressing love through a gift of time,
knitted yarn, and talent is never outdated.

All of our grandchildren have one of grandma's
special baby blankets designed to show her love.
I hope they'll keep and treasure it when
she's passed on to life in paradise up above.

She knits a special sweater for each child,
with buttons, pockets, and collars.
Such gifts are not replaceable, though
one spent a big pile of hard-earned dollars.

For her, knitting is a way to show love
without having to assemble the proper words.
I can only hope that the recipients get
the message that is demonstrated—not heard.

My wife understands that knitting
has a way of chasing the blues away.
When loving hands are busy, troubles
and worries just aren't able to stay.

With her hands, she demonstrates the love
that runs deeper than mere words can say.
Something handmade and usable is
a rare gift to receive in our present day.

I no longer laugh when I see older ladies
kibitzing and knitting away their free time.
I see it as an example of a love that
is enduring, wordless, and sublime.

Looking at Old Photos

A Story Poem

BY ALBEN CHAMBERLAIN

Who is that skinny, tow-headed boy
I see out on the lawn at play?
He certainly doesn't look anything
like I see reflected in a mirror today.

Who is that glum-looking boy with his
hair combed waiting for the school bus?
It might be me in another life, but I'm
not sure if, in my eyes, I can trust.

Who is that lean and tanned boy in the
sandlot with his baseball bat and glove?
If that was me, then how did all those
summer days fly away like a dove?

Is that really me holding a family dog
who left our lives so many decades ago?
That just might be me in another lifetime
the details of which I'll never know.

Who is that rail-thin ten-year-old on a
family vacation talking with cousins?
It must be me in a different lifetime,
but, then again, I think I've had dozens.

Who is that awkward nerdy teenager
without money, girlfriend, or a car?

When I try to retrieve all those old
memories, they've flown away too far.

Who is that lean and earnest young man
helping others far away in a foreign land?
I try to slow down every now and then to
recall those fading memories when I can.

Who is that starving-looking college student
standing by the bay on a Hawaiian beach?
Some of those memories I can still recall,
but most seem now, far beyond my reach.

Who is that serious-looking navy officer
standing at attention in his size 33 uniform?
Was that really me or was it taken in
another life from which I've been reborn?

Who is that dark-haired and newly married
man without a 2X shirt or a spare tire?
I can barely recognize that bloke now
that I'm old, overweight and retired.

Who is that earnest-looking young teacher
going off to teach in a public school?
That certainly looks like me, but, in
those days, I must have been a fool.

Who is that man who used to drive 2,000
miles in a month to make sales and earn respect?
It's hardly a person I recognize now that
I'm living on a microscopic pension check.

All of my teaching credentials and insurance licenses
have now lapsed, yet life is still moving on.
All of those faces looking out at me seem
like versions of me who are lost and gone.

Life is like a great river carrying my soul's
vessel farther down the rushing stream.
When I try to look back to where I was
before, it all seems just like a dream.

Cloud Alchemy

A Praise Poem

BY ALBEN CHAMBERLAIN

My wife is known
as the Sunset Queen
since she posts sunset pictures
on her Facebook page.
She's always looking for
just the right combination of
lowering sun and blocking cloud-
covering sun like a shroud.

A sunset without clouds
can be bold and dramatic,
yet it seldom has the
subtle tones of water vapor.
The declining sun hurls
its last golden spears
into luminous clouds-lighting
their underbellies with living color.

Scientists will describe it
all in technical terms
like reflection, refraction, and
energizing of atmospheric elements.
I prefer to view it
as a painter or master photographer
would-using a dozen words
to describe the subtle tones.

No. Basic red, orange, or yellow
aren't nearly enough colors.
Not when sunlight's alchemy
produces a hundred combinations.
The water molecules in
clouds appear to embrace the
fading sunlight like a lover
caressing it while it's present.

Just as no two clouds
are the same, no two
sunsets can be. Is this
beyond our human comprehension?
Sunlight and water molecules
never vary, though together
they create an alchemy
that thrills our souls.

My wife has posted
hundreds of sunset photos
over the years. Still,
each one shines unique.
Is that the secret
of human souls-all made
of common earth elements,
yet no two the same?

Kindergarten Teacher

BY NATALIE CHAMPION

I am a kindergarten teacher.

Students come with smiles, eager to learn.

They earn table points for good behavior, eagerly awaiting the
prizes they will choose from the prize box on Friday.

When I am feeling tired, their smiles energize me.

Sometimes it's not easy when they have to stay inside on a rainy day,

But it's always fun.

My students inspire me.

I love teaching kindergarten.

Calliope

by Rick Champion

I was meditating on the Irish Sea.

As a very young man I began to pick out tunes on my recorder. I dreamed of Shakespeare, and I hoped to learn the lute. Then I met *The Muse Calliope.*

At Berkeley I continued my autodidactic musical studies, usually under redwood trees and at dusk.

A friend played *Bach's Chaconne* on the guitar, and then, the Maglagueña.

A group of passing college women wondered where the music was coming from.

Fate had something in mind. I cried when I passed a music store on Haight St.

The three fates, Clotho, Lachesis and Atropos, who spin, draw out and cut the thread of Life, are the third subject in Petrarch's poem *The Triumphs.* First, Love triumphs; then Love is overcome by Chastity, Chastity by Death, Death by Fame, Fame by Time, and Time by Eternity.

On my horizon was a young girl – cute but shy. I went back to the waves. Young girl was giggles with eyes on me. Mama pushed, launching her my way.

The girl landed with a happy smile. "Hi", she said, right in my face, but friendly. She held up her hand. I held up mine. Friends in misfortune.

Mama grabbed an air guitar "We've thought of stringing the guitar differently."

I added, "I once heard musicians playing Appalachian music. The dulcimer player held a feather between her thumb and index finger. Her hands were burned."

The ship's loudspeaker demanded, "All off for Liverpool". I didn't want to lose my shelter for the night. As I moved to the exit, mama asked, "Is there anything that we can do for you?"

"Call my mom."

"But I don't know her."

"My mom will fill in all the gaps. Spend an hour. She has no off switch."

I went about my adventures forgetting the encounter. When I got home, my mom was proud.

"The girl's parents said that you were a nice young man. The parents worried about depression. They went to Europe to cheer her up, but nothing was working. Then she met you and saw that you were happy".

I had been through fire.

My mom went on, "They have a horse ranch near here. A forklift tipped over on her hand".

I never saw the girl or her mother again. I like to think that the hope lasted.

The Austrian pianist, Paul Wittgenstein, lost his right arm during World War I. He devised techniques that allowed him to play chords previously regarded as impossible for a five-fingered pianist.

Maurice Ravel composed (1929 and 1930) The Piano Concerto for the Left Hand in D Major.

African Mud Safari

by Sylvia Clarke

Alone on the campus up country
Wil at math conference in Dar
Good thing we have friends so nearby
Since here we don't have a car.

School's out—vacation time sighted.

"Let's go to the game park nearby."
Two families, two cars, I'm invited!
I won't need to stay home and cry.

Martha and children in one car
Dunder four in the other,
I take turns riding each vehicle
Sit by a sister or brother.

Road stretches out damp and rutted—
We're going in the "back way."
That means we must cross the river.
Will we get there yet today?

Recent rains here far from hidden
Road ahead plain out of sight.
"Get out and push," we are bidden.
I slosh my way to rear right.

"Ok, Push!" concerned driver calls.
Water, grass, mud start to fly.
My skirt already wet, dirty—
Cannot stay clean if I try!

Do it again with second car—
Slog through grass, water: be bold!
Had we even an inkling then
Of what the future might hold?

Late start and flooded conditions
We had not counted on—NO
Finding the right river crossing
Makes us much later and slow.

Twilight, preceding the darkness,
Shows us we'll be much too late
To find someone stationed there watching
To let us in at camp gate.

Suddenly the road's divided.
Should we take the left or right?
With the first car it's decided:
Oops! We are stuck for the night.

A tree blocks the road, and we find
Car axel in water, mud.
"Guess we camp here," we sigh, resigned.
"For fire, gather some wood!"

Eat something for our late supper
Build fire up strong and bright.
Sleep now mid-road near the fire
Discourage critters tonight.

Listen as herds thunder past us
Expect to hear lions instead
Of a child's sudden complaining,
"Who put a frog in my bed?"

Next, it's the snake that wiggles out
Of a log in the fire!
That makes us all heartily wish
Sleeping bags were up higher.

Morning reveals Hyena tracks
Up to puddle at our feet.
Glad we didn't know about it—
Or sleep would have been less sweet.

Pack up your gear! Douse the fire!
Light shows where to go and how.
Mud or not, praise goes up higher
Knowing God's still with us now.

Ageism?

BY SYLVIA CLARKE

I look in the mirror
surprised at what I see
That wrinkled old woman—
It just can't be me!

I clamber our hills
Walk our dog every day
May now amble slower
but still likes to play.

Smile with yellowed teeth
comb thinning grey hair
Find spots on arms and face—
how did they get there?

It's true I can't do
all I did with joy—
Hop, skip, jump over
or race a young boy,

But calling me old
before it's my time
Would not allow being
myself in my prime!

Do I judge myself
by our society—
Not seeing my value
or what I may be?

No, I must never

denigrate my worth!
Not just a number—
I belong on earth.

As one of God's children
I'm here for a reason
And while He directs me
I'll stay here my season!

First Acting Experience

BY SYLVIA CLARKE

Daddy is in a Temperance play and rehearsing at his college. The play is called "Prisoner at the Bar", and he is the Sheriff. At home he practices the song he sings at the end of the play:

> I dreamed that the great judgment morning
>
> Had dawned, and the trumpet had blown;
>
> I dreamed that the nations had gathered
>
> To judgment before the white throne;

He sings four verses with a chorus between. Daddy says there is a little girl in the play, but she can't sleep after practice and has bad dreams. They try another girl. She is also too young to take the tension of a murder trial, so, they look for someone else to take the part.

One morning Daddy tells me, "Sylvia, I suggested that you could probably play the little girl, Dorothy, the prisoner's daughter, in the play. Do you want to try?"

Be in a play? Yes! "Okay, Daddy," I answer. "What will I have to do?"

"You sit with Juanita—Mrs. Hall—and answer a few questions from the Judge. Then at one point you hug the man who plays your daddy. That's all."

That sounds easy enough. After all, I am seven-years-old and can do what I'm told—most of the time. The next rehearsal finds me with the other performers in a run-through, mostly for my sake. Since I do not have much to do and sleep okay afterwards, the leaders schedule a college chapel performance.

I really like Juanita—Mrs. Hall—that I sit next to, so that goes fine. I know how to answer the questions the Judge asks and relax until Mr. Richardson, who plays my—Dorothy's—dad breaks away to hug me and beg the Judge not to make me be a witness.

I have only met this man once before, so how can I hug him like I would my own Daddy? Somehow, I manage to put my arms around him—with my back to the audience. (A picture in the yearbook shows that.)

A few performances on the road at different churches and much changes. I learn to know and love Mr. Richardson as a friend since we all ride together in Mr. Kretschmar's big car. Besides, we perform the play over and over again. As time passes, I become less aware of the audience, and my hug in character as Dorothy grows more enthusiastic.

When Roscoe Nelson, my real Daddy, graduates, we move across the state. A few years later, a new pastor comes to our church. I'm excited because it's Pastor Estel Richardson, the very one who was Dorothy's dad in the play. I already know and love him, so I easily learn to love his family as well. That love started back in a Walla Walla College Temperance play where I had my first acting experience.

Lost—and Found

by Sylvia Clarke

"Don't forget this," I tell myself as I set my cell phone down. Then I attend to the business at hand. (Later I'm told I should always say, "Be sure to remember this!" instead.)

Wil and I are nearing the last homeward leg of our family reunion trip to North Carolina. We enjoy the scenery as we drive our Ford F150 west on state highways along the Platt River, through farmland in the plains, and over the Rocky Mountains. We treat ourselves with stops at National Parks and Monuments on the way. Today we stop at the Colorado end of Dinosaur National Monument to ask where we might camp for the night. The woman in the visitor's center is most helpful, and we come away with several brochures describing Bureau of Land Management areas—none of them nearby, however.

Driving across the state line into Utah, we head to visit the actual site where huge numbers of dinosaur bones were found. A bus ride from the visitor's center transports us to the building built over the hillside where many discoveries were made. It is most impressive. Inside we find huge leg bones, one standing upright taller than I, another providing a bench on which we sit and inspect the excavated wall with its embedded bone. Some of these are identified in signs along the railing. Behind us, several large displays depict the environments in which dinosaurs are thought to have lived. Smaller free-standing exhibits show skulls, vertebrae, or other bones of these extinct animals.

When we are ready to leave, the waiting bus driver kindly gives us a bottle we fill with water and drink. Having that drink of water allows us to take the half hour hike down a sunbaked trail to the visitor's center and our vehicle.

A day or so later I begin seriously looking for my phone. I've been thinking, "It must be here in the pickup somewhere," and hadn't needed it. Now, however, Wil tries calling it from his cell, but no hint of its ring reaches our ears. Now what?!

"Oh, no!" I groan. "My phone is lost? How will I get along without it? It has all my numbers!" Struggling to not worry, I silently pray, "Dear God, it's really your phone. So please look after it. I leave it in your hands."

As we visit Arches and Canyonlands National Parks over the next couple of days, I can revel in their natural beauty, taking short hikes between drives to the next popular spot. Then Wil gets a text from Uni, our daughter-in-law. "Fred [our son] called Mom's phone, and someone from Dinosaur Park answered. Here's a number to call."

I'm ecstatic! "How wonderful!" I cry out, "My lost phone is found! And I add a short prayer, "Thank you, God, for looking after it!"

Wil calls the number and talks with a park Ranger who says my phone is right there on his desk. I can't stop smiling. No more fighting off those worries about how I will reach my cousins or friends. Although these thoughts had not kept me awake at night, they often crossed my mind in daylight.

Three weeks later, the package with my cellphone arrives at our home. I praise God for watching over of it after my careless loss. What a trust-building experience—a demonstration that God truly cares!

King Solomon's Mines

by Wil Clarke

It was definitely not the best book I have ever read. I started reading before I went to school and read a lot of non-fiction, especially astronomy and ancient history, before I was twelve. When I turned twelve, my grandfather passed away from a stroke. He was 85. Within days of his passing my parents moved from South Africa to Southern Rhodesia. My parents packed my brother and me off to boarding school about 150 miles from home.

Up until this time, my parents had subtly discouraged my reading fiction. It doesn't fall under the Christian standard "Whatsoever things are true. ... Think on these things." Philippians 4:8. I was totally naïve about much of the world's reading tastes.

The boys' preceptor and one of my teachers in the seventh grade was Roy Naudé. Firstly, he knew my parents; secondly when he was about to punish my brother by beating him with a rounders bat, I had jumped between the two of them and forbade him from doing it. I think he marveled at my courage. He took an interest in me and encouraged me to broaden my reading. Since there was not much of a library, if any, at this little country boarding school, called Rhobecon Preparatory School, he loaned me H. Rider Haggard's *King Solomon's Mines*. It had the advantage of describing life in rural Africa, mainly from an adventurer's point of view, of course. It was written around the turn of the 20th century, was exciting to any boy, and definitely fiction.

The book tells the tale of three adventurers, Allan Quartermain, Sir Henry Curtis, and Captain Good, who chase out across the desert to try and find the fabled King Solomon's Mines, where the best gold was there for the taking. After nearly dying while crossing the terrible desert, they cross a mountain range and come into a verdant country. Most of the people accept them, but the old hag, Gagool, scuttles the whole thing and they barely escape with their lives and very little treasure. I sometimes wonder if Google is a name inspired by the old witch and not the mathematical term "googol".

This introduced me to the joy of reading, purely for the excitement it gives. Subsequently, when we moved to a place near a library, in England no less, I took to reading other Haggard novels—all taking place in Africa. Somehow, I also picked up on reading Dickens, like *A Tale of Two Cities*. I liked him, even though he is far wordier than Haggard and apparently hardly knows that Africa exists. Like Churchill, Dickens was paid by the word, so if he could squeeze a few more words into his stories, he made more money. I don't remember the first time I read *A Christmas Carol*, but I ended up reading the book to my kids during many a Christmas season. They would ask me to do so even in years after they were grown and knew the story back to front. Our daughter, Julia, took us to a *Christmas Carol* play last December at A Noise Within Theatre in Pasadena, for the fourth time! And we've loved it every time. It's nice to be able to know the next words the actor is going to say!

If and When I Raise Children

by Wil Clarke

When children develop the power to reason from cause to effect, I would try to reason with them before punishing them.

You've been in a public place when you've heard a parent yell: "Ephraim get your buns over here!" And she does it again and again, and finally chases Ephraim and then yanks his arm almost out of its socket and swats his behind. No wonder the kid didn't come! He knew full well what the treatment was going to be!

I watched this happen to young Johnny. He was probably eight years old, the son of a missionary family who lived next to us on the mission station in Africa. He had gotten to the point where he spoke back to his parents in the same tone they used on him.

I took a couple of neighbor kids on a mile walk to a giant pile of rocks to do some scrambling on them. We got out on a flat rock separated from the other rocks by a 15-foot-deep chasm. I stood with one foot on one side of the chasm and the other foot on the other side and helped those who wanted help across. Now we were on an island in the air. Roger and Neil, children of another missionary family, let their imaginations soar. Being the youngest, Johnny came up with some imaginary scenarios that gave him and everyone there a sense of power and accomplishment.

Then we all decided we had had enough and started to leave, that is all except Johnny. He was having too much fun in his imagination. I again straddled the chasm and helped each one that needed it, across. But Johnny stood there and ranted and raved at me like he did to his parents. Finally, I said firmly, "Johnny, if you don't come now, we will leave you here and you will have to get yourself down."

We climbed on down the rocks and I entered the chasm and stood below where Johnny would have to cross, in case he actually tried it and fell, I would catch him. But we were sufficiently hidden so that he couldn't see us. Furthermore, he was too scared to try to cross it by himself.

He continued his ranting and raving for a couple minutes.

When he no longer could see us, nor hear us, he grew quiet. Then we could hear him start to call me. Then he started to cry and sob. He could have easily stepped across the chasm, but his fear had frozen him and then morphed into panic.

Although it was only five minutes or so, it seemed like eternity to Johnny, I walked back up on the top of the giant boulders. After helping him across, I said quietly, "You know Johnny, when you're doing things with me, it is very important that we work together."

I was in charge of the physical plant of the mission we were on. This took me all over the surrounding area. After that Johnny came with me a lot. He enjoyed doing the things I was doing. Never again did he speak to me in the rebellious tones he still used on his parents. Later I spoke to his parents and asked them what he had told them about the climbing event. He had told them nothing, but the joy he had experienced. He is now well up in his fifties, a successful radio and TV announcer. He still rejoices to see me when I'm in the DC area.

In that case, a little firm reasoning worked wonders in his life.

Miss Winkler

by Wil Clarke

I started school in Standard 1 in 1950 at Helderberg Primary School, in South Africa. In those semi-barbaric days, the common punishment for boys was a whipping—we called it "cuts"—administered by a teacher or the principal who wielded a wicked cane onto the boy's buttocks. It stung like a dozen wasp stings, and left angry black and blue welts across the width of the backside.

When I was in Standard 5, 1954, I was placed in Miss Winkler's class. This news came with a certain amount of trepidation. She was known to have a nasty temper. I was a good student and usually tied with Margie McClure for being the best student in the class, so I wasn't really worried. I worked hard and kept my homework up to date, so I didn't fear her ire very much.

One day, however, I did something—to this day, I have no clue what it was—that Miss Winkler took umbrage at. She descended on me, yelling at me. She grabbed the one-foot wooden ruler lying on my desk. Then she started beating me across my back and my shoulders then across my head and face. One blow sent my glasses flying across the room. A gasp of horror went around the classroom. They, too, had no idea what I had done to elicit her rage. They were in mortal fear that they might be the next one to get it. I was totally humiliated and mortified.

Dad, a veteran teacher, always wanted to support other teachers. He told me when I first started school in Standard 1, that if I ever got a spanking at school, I would get a second one from him when I came home. I entered home that day in fear of a further beating from him. I said nothing about the event. Dad was teaching in Helderberg High School and College, so he quickly got the news that I had been punished in school. When he came home that evening, he looked at me and asked, "Did you get a spanking from Miss Winkler, today?"

"Y y y Yes," I stammered, both embarrassed and afraid.

"You remember the understanding we had when you first started school?"

I nodded, still too embarrassed to say more.

"Alright, come into the bathroom." He reached behind the bathroom door and took his heavy double leather razor strap off its hook. "Bend over!"

I did and he walloped my backside several blows. I felt dreadfully alone. My school friends were too scared to say anything to me, lest they would also get chastised. And now, Dad had beaten me, too. That was Monday or Tuesday.

On Friday, Dad came home and straight to me. He sat down and asked, "Did Miss Winkler beat you across your face?"

"Yes!" I answered hesitantly. When I saw that he was no longer angry at me, the whole story tumbled out.

"I wish you had said something!" He said apologetically. "I never would have spanked you! I'm sorry!"

That was the end of that agreement. He never mentioned it to my younger brother. Later that year my folks moved to a remote mission station in another country and I went to boarding school for the rest of my junior and senior high school years. I had at least two teachers who were openly sadistic and I got caned frequently. One of the teachers beat me until blood flowed down my legs. If that agreement had still been in effect I would probably have never gone home. My life would be wildly different today.

After more than sixty years, I saw Margie a couple years ago. She asked me if I remembered that event. She didn't remember what I had done to make Miss Winkler so angry either. She said she lived in fear and trembling the rest of the year lest she should get beaten like I had. Miss Winkler was removed from her position a few years later.

Sacred Instrument

by James Coats

The beat begins to bounce
then the soul starts to sync,
ears tickled by the teasing electric atmosphere
while the rhythm rises through the blood.
The body initiates a conversation with itself
in the form of a dancing drum composition.
Hair running wild as recess.
Eye close to catch the essence of sound.
Head shimmies causing the neck and spine
to snake in upright position
calling shoulders to shift smooth as a new clutch.
Arms twist up and around as tree vines
reaching for the sky then back down across the ribs
spreading like roots digging through musical waves.

Stomach tightens and pulls, core stretches
asking hips to turn and swivel, left then right
cyclone rotations causing thighs to lift and fall.
Pillars of powerful motion like an old locomotive
thighs request the knees to drop it low
knees say *we'll only drop it halfway.*
Butt cheeks question how much shaking
will be required of them tonight.
Calves admire how good they look in the club's glow
while doing the least amount of effort.
Feet fluttering wings, slightly skimming the floor
ankles sweet jelly spreading back and forth.
All while hands scoop musical passion into chest
lungs exhausted, breathing heavy.
My brain wonders why are we even up
past our bedtime.

Mirror Mirror

BY JAMES COATS

If I were making my own mirror
I don't think the reflection would look like me.
I'd add to the parts I want to improve
and take away from parts that I detest.
I wish this body could replicate
how I felt inside,
that my strength of will
could manifest in strength of body.
I'd read book after book on techniques
to get the best reflection I could
double and triple checked the math,
but after every attempt I still
always ended up with me.

As if God was telling me:
Why are you trying to change
what I already created
the way you should be?

But I can't believe his message
I have seen his work first hand.
So I smash the glass to pieces
pick up the largest shards cut my hand on it.
Contemplate slicing three inches higher
so I won't have to start over again.

Maybe, the one ingredient,
in the process I forgot was self-love.
Begin to fashion enough self-esteem
to be grateful with the way I came out,
because imperfect doesn't equal wrong
and a broken body can still feel joy,

can still be seen as a desirable thing
despite its different functioning.
Perhaps, I'll stop letting others teach
me how to be my own creator.

Growing up when I was in the way, mom would say
your daddy wasn't a glass maker
but maybe she didn't know him that well
because I've always felt so invisible inside.
A soul with no sliver of silver to shine against
only a transparent portal, petri dish of pain.

Cartoon Deer in Headlights

BY ELINOR COHEN

I wasn't getting anywhere with my writing assignment, sitting sideways hunched over a blank page in my notebook. I tried chanting a little mantra to get me started, but it turned into a clumsy high-low melody that only distracted me further. I put down my pen and walked outside.

I was looking around for inspiration, or maybe just looking around, when I noticed the very lopsided car parked in the carport behind me. It was Hot Neighbor Guy's maroon SUV, recognizable by the "My Other Car Is The Batmobile" bumper sticker, but the whole right side was absolutely destroyed. Bits of shredded rubber where the tires should be, bits of shredded metal where the wheels should be. Scratches like claw marks on the lower part of the door frame. What made those marks? Bird talons? A chainsaw? I imagined Hot Neighbor Guy (HNG from now on) minding his own business, cruising down the highway listening to the Grateful Dead, as one does, when suddenly a giant pterodactyl swooped down from the Jurassic Era and took a big gnarly swipe! Or maybe it was a road rage incident involving the post-apocalyptic porcupine truck from Mad Max with the spikes on the wheels, and what if HNG got too close, and what if Mad Max hates the Grateful Dead?

I breathed in and out. Something bad happened here.

I wondered if HNG was okay. I wondered if his Stupid Hot Wife was okay. Her shiny black Mercedes kingpin car wasn't parked in the spot next to his. Standing there staring, I saw a sheet of paper taped to the window that read: "Car will be towed away on Monday, sorry for the eyesore." I chuckled, not because it was funny, but because the word 'eyesore' always makes me think of Eeyore, the deeply depressed donkey from the Winnie the Pooh crew, and I remembered reading a random fan theory online that claimed Eeyore is so gloomy because he's Christopher Robin's least favorite toy, backed by the indisputable fact than an unappealing stuffed donkey, a literal jackass, doesn't have the familiar human resemblance of an upright bear.

So I stood there staring and chuckling for an inappropriately long time, until the driver's side door opened and HNG got out of the car! He was sitting in there the whole time I was playing Worst Case Scenario with his life! Shit! I was caught. I froze in place with my mouth hanging open for half a minute like a cartoon deer in headlights. He looked over at me and we locked eyes. I panicked and blurted out the first dumb thing that popped into my head, like I tend to do when I'm uncomfortable.

"Did a bear attack your car?"

"No my wife" he replied, in a near whisper.

"A bear attacked your wife?" I blurted.

"My wife attacked my car" was his response.

Nothing, I said, or rather, I said nothing, and I never spoke another word again, ever, to anyone, to this day. I had no words. From the shock of it. The total shock. And the horror. And the little bit of delight? What, no that's completely terrible. Bad bad. All bad. And maybe hilarious? Shut up, I told the drama-loving devil on my shoulder, as I tried to make my face look sad.

"She might be my ex-wife now" HNG said and started to cry. Or was he laughing? Then he turned around and went into his house.

I stood there until the anxiety-induced paralysis wore off. Then I turned around and went into my house. Right across from his. Where I promptly fainted.

Waiting Room

BY ELINOR COHEN

So many stories percolating in the doctor's office waiting room today.

There was the guy who had to arrive an hour early because he needed a Valium to get through whatever procedure he had scheduled, and the nurse insisted on being the one who administered it. And I mean, that's cool, but people still take Valium? This dude asked for it by name. I would love a freaking Valium, it would be a nice mellow throwback compared to the high dose Xanax I have hidden at home for anxiety emergencies.

There was the man in a wheelchair with an oxygen nose hose who repeatedly complained that he couldn't breathe, until his possibly murderous younger wife lifted her heavy leather bag off of his oxygen tube on the floor. Unintentionally murderous you say? Not too sure. That suspiciously placed bag was big. Big like the baseball cap he was wearing with a visor that came down too low in the front, probably so his mean wife didn't have to make eye contact with him.

Then, too, the woman who came gliding gracefully down the carpeted hallway with her walker, one of those fancy walkers that turns into a little chair for when you've absolutely had enough and need to sit and rest real quick. She said her name loudly at the check-in desk: Rosemary Ritter. Possibly of the infamous Hollywood Ritters? Related to Tex? John? Jason? Ok here's a workaround riddle to avoid a lawsuit in case I'm wrong: classic Country Western singer whose son was a Trip[per] who drank at the Beagle and shared a name with the Ripper, and *his* son is a crooked man who didn't probably save the world and whose wife is also married to the king of the world in the one with Meryl Streep about the end of the world. Got it? The internet sleuths reading my future bestseller will.

Someone started humming softly in the corner. What fresh hell is this? Humming in public? I do not approve of this behavior. Only serial killers whistle and hum in crowded rooms. But wait, I know this song… Mr. Sandman, bring me a dream (dun dun dun dun) make him the cutest that I've ever seen (dun dun dun dun)… I caught myself before I tapped my toe to the tune but I did accidentally bob my head one time.

When the serial killer stopped his infernal buzzing, it got super quiet. Maybe I could take a quick nap, just for a minute? I was wearing dark prescription sunglasses so it would be hard for these other people to tell if my eyes were open or closed. I was also wearing a surgical mask over my mouth and nose, and if I pulled the hood of my sweatshirt up over my head, nobody would be able to decipher my deal at all. Fully incognito. I'm gonna do it. Sleep in the waiting room. While I wait. Could I get comfortable on this sturdy pleather chair? I stared at the gigantic TV screen placed awkwardly in the middle of the room and wondered if it used to be an aquarium because I feel like maybe it used to be an aquarium and if that's true, they should definitely make it be one again because watching fish swim around in circles lowers my blood pressure. And that would help me fall asleep.

Moments? later? A while later? I was awakened by a deep gravelly voice declaring "Africa is only one percent vaccinated did you know that for the covid." Oh no. This could be bad. Is there a bathroom I could go stand in front of or a supply closet I could hide in? Gravelly Lady continued "yeah they're only one percent vaccinated over down there in Africa and whose fault is that if not the rest of the selfish goddamn world." Oh okay. Her skinny friend looked moderately mortified and said: Haha how about we concentrate on filling out these forms— or something, whatever, I stopped listening after that and diligently played Solitaire on my phone.

My mother emerged after an eternity, with a neon pink bandage around her arm and an exasperated look on her face. In the car on the way home I told her about the Valium guy and she whipped around in her seat all excited and said "I saw him back there, and I saw them give him the Valium, and they said they were going to monitor him in another room, and I said, gee, people still take Valium?"

I thought about the terribly uninteresting waiting room conversation my mom and I had earlier, that someone else was forced to overhear. A partial transcript: "You know how when you order Chinese take-out, you always get a fortune cookie? Well why don't other ethnic food restaurants send you home with a tiny free dessert? Like why doesn't Chipotle slip you a miniature churro or a couple of cinnamon chips? That Greek place should pop a sticky bite of baklava in the bag. And if you order from a Barbecue joint, you should get a little fire-roasted marshmallow, or fuck it, get the whole s'more. But I'm kind of stuck on Chipotle or like Castaneda's with its 24-hour drive-thru and weird flan. Speaking of Mexican food, I've finally realized after all these many years that bruschetta is literally just salsa for Italians. Ah it sounds so funny when you say 'brus-ket-a' when I've been calling it 'brush-shet-a' my whole life. Anyway when those clever Romans realized that cilantro tastes like dirty dish soap, they replaced it with the far superior herbaceous basil. But the guy at Mario's still doesn't toss me a baby cannoli when I order my ziti to go. Is this conversation racist? Do *you* think this conversation is racist?" Etc. etc.

John Ritter's mom's name was Dorothy Fay. I googled it as soon as I got home. She starred in a bunch of Western movies in the 1930s and '40s, and moved into the Motion Picture & Television Country House and Hospital in 1989 after suffering a stroke. She died in 2003 at the age of 88, less than two months after John. Bummer. The woman I casually stalked was a rando.

P.S. Shoutout to the fabulously dressed woman in a different doctor's office waiting room a week ago who yelled at the Desk

Ladies crouched behind clear panes of plexiglass: "What do you mean my insurance might not cover this? Do you know who I am? I used to be the mayor of Beverly Hills! Yes I was! It was my idea to give every resident 2 free gigabytes of internet way back before Netflix started streaming movies in every home! Yes I did! That was me! And you know what else? I'm a breast cancer survivor, and that diagnosis was the best thing that ever happened to me, because I had massive breast reduction surgery and now I can stand up straight without any back pain!" And then she said, quieter: "This bottle of water you gave me to drink is beyond undrinkable, don't you have anything more expensive?"

My Mother's Love

BY ALBERT CONTRERAS

If I only had my mother to bring a present to,
I wouldn't pick just Mother's Day, but any day would do.
I wish I had her here with me to tell her how I love her.
I'd tell her what she meant to me for she was like no other.

She always had a smile for me, she always understood
I did no wrong as she could see like no other mother could.
I envy every mother here — when they have sons who love her.
I only wish that mine were here — my precious loving mother.

No other love is greater than Jesus' love for me,
But my mother's love is closest than any love could be.
So tell her what she means to you, on this her special day.

I only wish that mine were here,
    But, she has passed away.

Note: Albert's poem was inspired by a request of his minister, Pastor James Ritch of the Four Square Church in La Puente, California.

Delicacy

BY CARLOS E. CORTÉS

The two crabby Canadian geese
Strode defiantly alongside Laurel
Imprisoning
As they maneuvered her around Lake Evans
To make certain that
She didn't go near their little ones
Protecting the less-than-eighty-days
From the more-than-eighty-years
Not knowing that we sometimes eat fowl

The ominous saltwater crocodile
Glared defiantly
Through the hopefully thick glass
At the Singapore Zoo
Inches from our faces
Then opened its enormous jaws
To display those ancient teeth
Before he swung his tail
And thrashed away
Not knowing that we had eaten "salties" for lunch

So what should I say
To our neighbor's poodle
Not knowing that I had enjoyed
A savory lunch
In Seoul, South Korea,
Before I discovered
What I had eaten

With a Side Order of Noise

BY CARLOS E. CORTÉS

Laurel's mouth moved
But no sound emerged as her
    Leaping hands
    Glistening eyes
    Animated smile
Told me that she was saying something interesting
Yet I couldn't hear

Because some dork in the darkening restaurant
Had suddenly turned on music
    Blaring
    Intrusive
    Uninvited
In the middle of our half-eaten anniversary dinner
While we were enjoying lamb chops
And each other, until . . .

"Could you please turn off the music
Or at least turn it way, way down?
I can't hear a word my wife is saying."

The manager,
Perplexed that I would rather talk to Laurel
Than listen to his recorded noise,
Stared at me, disbelieving.

"I'll give you two choices, Mr. Manager.
We can leave now without paying for what we've already

eaten and drunk . . .
Or you can turn off the blasting music
until we finish our dinner.
Then you can bombard everyone else's ear drums
If that's why they really came here."

The manager wavered,
Unaccustomed to facing a resolute 88-year-old
Who was damned if he was going to lose any more
Of his declining hearing that night
And didn't care if he made a scene.

Platitudes of an Orange

BY CAIT DANIELLE

An orange does not know
how I think of it,
or that I picked this one as best,
and cannot mind me at all
when I puncture my thumb
through its navel,
calloused skin against
calloused skin.

I wish my clementine would know
how I kept its dignity.
How carefully I inched my finger
under its rind, trying my best
to peel in one steady strand.
Or how the pith stained my nail
even after I scooped it out
with the front of my tooth
and swallowed its absent platitudes.

Wildflower(fire)

by Cait Danielle

Between highway divider and big rig, we take a chance on tire debris,
    and I imagine this is how roadkill goes,
a brief moment of acceptance before one side of the car rises
    and falls.

We pull over, the wildfire now far from us, but still trapping smoke
    in the valley.
Arms covered in soot, knuckles scraping against
    rubber, I unbolt what once protected us, now

dragging us down. Gravel imprints my knees.
    I have never felt more like myself.
A wildflower growing from a car tire, sweat unabsorbed, smoke
    soaking the sun in red.

Muse

by Cait Danielle

Within a haze of empty pages,
    I suggest that we fuck all night.
Try out this age-old idea that I have considered a myth,
    that I have not wanted to consider at all.
Undress me and watch me
     make words from movement,
from desperation. Watch them spring from my head
    like they were waiting for *this* love.
Let it be you who is my muse, show me that I am worthy
    of one, that I am still a poet.

Rewilding

BY CAIT DANIELLE

Above the bathroom mirror
where I face myself naked,
the Santa Ana winds tear
the tarp from my roof,
and I consider not caving into myself,
not by wind, nor water, nor reflection.

When the wind soothes to only a breath,
I go for a walk.
The house near the park
is rewilding, saying, *do not touch me*
and see how I grow.

See how I unfold, too,
like tendrils from my garden,
where aloe vera heaves
through cement blocks,
where sprigs of lavender

droop in the evening's shade
like a head bobbing through
dream cycles,
dreams of breath unshaken,
a constant cool breeze

begging to fill the space
between bare skin and soil.

My First Job – 7-27-2022

by Chuck Doolittle

If you're old enough, you'll remember the lines at the gas pump back in '73 and '74. License plates that ended with odd numbers were entitled to a maximum of 10 gallons of gas only on odd numbered days of the week. In turn, plates ending in even numbers were permitted the same amount on even numbered days. What you might not remember, is the young kid, seemingly uneasy, dealing with customers short on patience, who often demanded more fuel than allowed. That kid was me.

It was my first job. A long time built up to it delivering newspapers and mowing lawns. But this one was the "real" first job. The kind that involves an application, interview, a uniform, weekly work schedule, training, a weekly check, and oh yeah, a boss!

My boss's name was Clarence Hubble and the gas station's name was Hubble's Exxon. It was situated on the corner of two busy streets, Sixth and Main, in Corona, CA. Mr. Hubble was a tad eccentric, and quite likely a bit of a drinker. He often showed up for work appearing slightly hungover, his face flushed, often in a mood to match. He could be completely entertaining, life of the party type one minute, and be yelling at you for nothing of significance the next. There was never a dull moment at Hubble's Exxon. On a good day, he'd have the employees, all three of us, one mechanic and two attendants, come to the service bay and he'd grab a bunch of tire valve stems. He would then challenge us to see if any of us, including himself, could kick one all the way to Sixth Street. It was a royal waste of time but loads of fun. That's how I prefer to remember Mr. Hubble.

The job entailed pumping gas, washing windows, checking under the hood, checking tire pressure, and handling money. We also were trained to do minor car repairs and maintenance, such as oil changes, lubes, repair flats, and clean out the oil pit. That last one was a gross and extremely disgusting job that I detested. All in all, for a guy who liked people, liked cars, and liked to work, it was a perfect job. But not always.

Occasionally, there were scalding, hot radiators that required water, spewing steam like locomotives. In those days, the actual radiator cap had to be removed, doing so was an art and science all in one. It required a multi-step process: using a thick rag to cover the cap, turning the cap while pressing down on it simultaneously, and doing so slowly enough for the pressure to escape gradually until released. That was the ideal, anyway.

One day two cute girls drove up needing help. Upon closer inspection, I noticed they were wearing bathing suits. The steam emitting from that engine's hood was reminiscent of Old Faithful. They smiled while asking me to check it. The aforementioned art and science involved in this process were only as good as the focus of the person attempting it. Let's just say my focus was a bit distracted at that moment. In the time it took to say "hey" to two cute girls, that radiator exploded, leaving second and third degree burns up the lower half of my arm. It was definitely one of the most painful lessons I'd ever learned.

Another time, my fellow attendant and I both thought the other had put oil back into a car after changing it. When I proceeded to start it, Greg could be heard shouting, "There's no oil. There's no oil!" Sixteen-year-olds and their first jobs. How did employers put up with us? Mine did until he didn't.

My second to last day of my two-year gas station attendant stint involved a man who paid with an expired credit card. In those days, pumping came first and payment came last. All I could do was recognize that it was expired, which I did, and tell the man I was going to have to keep it, which I also did. But that wasn't good enough for Mr. Hubble. The next day when I arrived to work, Mr. Hubble was sitting at his desk doing the books. He called me in, and it was apparent he wasn't happy. He didn't care for my handling of the expired card. I asked him what I should have done instead, and he never gave any logical explanation, instead informing me that I no longer had a job. I'd obviously caught him on one of his bad days, and there was no arguing with him. At those times, it was his way or the highway. Off toward the highway I went.

Mr. Hubble died a few years later. I was sad to hear it. Regardless of him being a rather difficult man, I'd always think of him kindly. I loved that job and always will. The life lessons and experiences I garnered are with me still. So much learned, both good and bad, accompanying me down life's path.

The Cruelty of Taxation

by Chuck Doolittle

I'll tax your shoes and tax your booze
Your house, your car, your caviar,
I'll not ask nicely, not ask at all
You'll hand it over at my beckon call.
Your savings, investments, your future is mine,
I'll take it and drink it like a glass of wine.
But wait, aren't there loopholes to ease all the pain?
That's when I attack you with capital gains.
But one thing that's offered are dangling tax breaks
Amounting to nothing cause I'll takes what I takes
Your stocks, your bonds, your IRAs
Are barely a pittance when I take my raise
Try running, they say, across the state line,
I'm delighted, for you see, that's the ultimate fine.
Hear you'll be marrying, isn't that sweet,
I'll happily tax the honeymoon suite.
Your first house, how cute, with the white picket fence.
Makes me ecstatic, property taxes are immense.
Have children, it's said, it'll reduce what you pay
Better read the fine print, I'll get you some way
Congratulations, you've arrived, to the tax deductions,
All part of the plan, the ultimate seduction.
For you see there is really no way to be free,
Uncle Sam does not allow for autonomy.
But finally, you think you're safe when you're not,
The taxes run freely for the coffin and the plot.

—Inspired by "Taxman", The Beatles, 1966

The Man Was No Myth

by Chuck Doolittle

If you were told that Martin Luther King Jr. and Robert Kennedy were assassinated and man orbited the moon for the first time in the same year, would you be able to name it? Okay, if that's too hard, what if I told you it was also the year my sister graduated from high school? Not much help? Lest you are chomping at the bit with anticipation, I will end your suffering. The year was 1968. Yes, two of the country's most influential men of the time were tragically struck down in their prime. On December 21, Frank Borman and James A. Lovell became the first astronauts to orbit the moon in Apollo 8. And, yes, though likely less eventful, my sister completed her public-school education the same year. But in my sixth grade, 11-year-old mind, none of these events were as memorable as the impression left on me by one man.

Mr. Compton was my science and math teacher at Lincoln Elementary School in Corona, California. A group of about 60 of us were tracked since fourth grade after having been identified as GATE students. The program consisted of attending three different schools for 4th, 5th, and 6th grades, presumably to be offered the most highly qualified teachers. I couldn't tell you who my 4th and 5th grade teachers were. I guess that says something in itself. But then came 6th grade.

Mr. Compton was exceptional in every way. He possessed the gift of being relatable to everyone, and he had the cool "it-factor" that commanded respect. He regarded us as intelligent, evident in his teaching style. His class taught me the intricacies of dissecting and identifying the parts of a shark. He would circulate during his science lessons, motivating us to excel. He was the kind of teacher you just wanted to please. If he complimented you, which he often did, it made your day. I recall craving his approval. I also remember him challenging us unlike any other teacher had. He routinely expected what seemed insurmountable, yet he instilled in us self-confidence that made us feel well-equipped. I found myself excited to get to school, wondering what we'd encounter that day. His class never disappointed. One day during winter, Corona received a rare dusting of snow that occurred during class. We jumped out of our seats and ran outside to a nearby stretch of grass in between the buildings. He not only allowed it, he joined in the frolic. We might not have felt so free to do that with another teacher. But with Mr. Compton, we knew different. But, wow, did that year fly by.

The end of school field trip was fitting. While not unusual for a teacher to take a class to a movie for a culminating activity, there was nothing usual about Mr. Compton's movie choice. We attended the premiere of *2001: A Space Odyssey*. It was two hours and 19 minutes, which was long for my attention span, and the content was deep. Now, maybe it was just me, but I walked out of the theater that day wondering what I'd just seen. It was far over my 11-year-old head. But, looking back on it, that's how Mr. Compton taught. He constantly gave us something to think about. He convinced us that we had brains and he wanted us to use them, and to remember that when we moved on.

I reflect fondly on the year 1968. Though turmoil, strife, new discoveries, and high school graduations abounded, my experience had a singular focus. It was placed on the man that gave of himself, for the sake of his students, that we might better ourselves, and maybe, just maybe, go forth and make the world a better place.

Ziona

by Reiss DuPlessis

We met when we were freshmen in college. The development of our friendship was immediate. She was one of my fraternity brother's girlfriend. She became more like a sister than he was, ever, a brother. Interestingly and, somewhat sadly, many years later, she would tell me I was more her brother than was her only brother by birth. For some reason, fate deigned we meet, become lifelong friends, confidants and never, for a moment, see that special bond weakened or threatened. We loved each other as good friends do but, more importantly, we respected and liked each other. We had no secrets, were known to talk out each other's concerns and problems into the wee hours of the morning and never, in a friendship that lasted to the day she died of breast cancer in her sixties, did we ever have a serious argument. A lifetime after our meeting and years after her loss, I try to understand how and why our friendship was so strong, so powerful and indestructible. I think, the first reason was the respect I had for her brain power. To say she was brilliant is selling her short. She had reasoning powers superior to most, shared my interests in music, books, arts and crafts, philosophy and world issues. I felt, to the day I lost her, that she was the person to whom I could always turn to discuss, investigate or solve any issue or problem. I can, without doubt, say she and my siblings were my best teachers, coaches, mentors and friends… ever.

When she and Irv married, I was a groomsman in their wedding that took place at sunset in the outdoor area of her synagogue in the San Fernando Valley. What a joyful evening! I had never danced the Hora before but loved every step. I maintained a close friendship with them even when their marriage began to stumble. I found myself listening to both sides of their problems and fought like hell to remain objective. Unfortunately, while I liked Irv and kept our friendship alive, when it came time to meet in the divorce court, I was her witness. Somehow, that did not destroy my friendship with Irv but, after the divorce, she remained part of my life and, even, part of my family. Irv moved in other directions. We still, however, shared an occasional phone conversation. Indeed, when, all those years later, he had another wife and family, it was I who called to tell him of Ziona's death.

Ziona and I shared an interest and love of folk music. It was she who convinced me I should buy a guitar because, it would be easier to sing with the guitar than the piano. Neither of us knew I would, in time, with my trusted guitar, perform folk music in Lovys and Eddie's troupe called Hollywood Presents and later, find myself singing around the area represented by Karoon who usually represented Middle Eastern dancers. Many of the songs I sang during my gigs were ones I learned from Ziona.

I grew up in a very Catholic city, family and schools. I, when I got to college, developed an interest in world religions. Indeed, one of my favorite classes in my second year of college was one on comparative religions. Ziona became my teacher about the world of Judaism. In my fourteen years in Catholic schools, I had learned nothing about Judaism or the Holocaust, so I was curious beyond imagining when Ziona began my education of that horrific period of history. She told me stories about friends and relatives' experiences and, eventually, introduced me to several survivors of the nightmares that were the concentration camps in which millions of people died. Needless to say, at eighteen and nineteen years of age, I was astounded and even angry that this had happened and that I had not been informed about it in my, otherwise, fairly good education.

Life has exposed me to people from many walks of life. I have friends and acquaintances from around the globe. To say I have had a good and colorful life in more truth than fiction. Today, I am older, slightly better informed but not necessarily wiser because I still suffer the naïveté of youth and am astounded by some of the realities in our world. Sadly, I don't have Ziona with whom to discuss that world.

Winners and Losers

BY JERRY ELLINGSON

Running can be about winners and losers. But, it's about more than that. It was the "more than that" that was a gift I experienced when I trained for my first marathon with the L.A. Roadrunners as an overweight, out of shape, 57 year old woman.

Our coach was retired. He had competed in the Olympics as a marathon runner in his younger years. As a young man he joined the Los Angeles Police Department. His job was to train the new recruits to be physically fit. What he explained to us, over and over, was that it isn't about the winning or losing, but about achieving your personal best. With over 1,200 members, we were a big presence running along Venice Beach every Saturday morning. We were in it for the long haul. We wanted to accomplish the end result of completing 26.2 miles on Marathon Day. To think that you need to run ahead of the pack every time you run, just to win, would keep you from completing your goal. I'm so grateful we had such a wise man to lead us.

Of course, not everyone training for, and participating in the Marathon was part of Roadrunners, so we encountered some real jerks in our eight months of training, as we traveled our own trails during the week, but we all just kept on following coaches instructions and we all were able to finish.

One day, about a third of the way into training, my husband told me that, Bob, a friend of ours, asked if we could meet for brunch one Sunday. He wanted to talk to me about my training program. Bob was younger than us. He was in his early 40s, tall, and a good looking man. He was an undercover police officer. Sometimes, when undercover, he didn't look like the above description. The day we met for brunch at a very nice restaurant, Bob had shaggy hair and a mangy beard. He and his wife had also arrived in the old, undercover van that was shabby inside and out. The paint was oxidized and rusted in spots. I wasn't even sure what color it might have been when it was new. It was dented and the only windows it had were the front and side windows in the front of the van. If he hadn't been with his wife, I wouldn't have recognized our friend, who grew up on the Coast, had known everyone in his small, affluent community since he was a little boy, owned a yacht and belonged to a prestigious yacht club.

At brunch, Bob told me that he worked in a team with three other officers. They worked nights. One of the men was a runner. He ran every morning at four or five o'clock when they finished their shift. He wanted to run the L.A. Marathon and he wanted the others in his team to run it with him.

I explained that they were getting a late start, but told him that I would give them all of my schedules and informational papers from the first day I began training. If they had any questions or injuries as they trained, I would get information for them from the expert staff available to us at all times. I told him where to go to be fitted properly for running shoes, how to bandage his toes to prevent black toe, to use band aids on his nipples to prevent bleeding, and everything else I could think of that he might need to know. Bob made it very clear during that first day of conversation that he didn't want to do this. He was only doing it for the others in his team. I assured him that it would be a great experience.

We got together often, as training progressed. I gave him copies of my training sheets and information on slight injuries any of them were experiencing. It was during one of these meetings, that Bob told me the runner in his team who had insisted they all run the marathon was very competitive and cocky. He didn't want to take any advice from a woman, especially an "old" woman. He did his own thing, sometimes running in the morning after work with the guys, but ignoring any information I was sharing with them. The other three followed the schedules I gave them every week.

After the marathon we went to lunch with Bob and his wife again. I was so excited to hear about his marathon day. He said the four of them lined up together for the start. The runner that insisted they all participate in the marathon with him, wanted to start off fast. The other three, having followed all of the training information, knew that wasn't a wise move. The trio stayed together the whole race while their fourth partner sprinted ahead, on his own. They all finished the race, but the trio finished about an hour and a half earlier than their fourth partner. While they waited for their last man to finish, they discussed how irritated and disgusted they were with the antics of this guy that had pushed himself forward as a seasoned runner, while he considered them to be just amateurs. But, then they came to the very wise conclusion that they were a team, and instead of ridiculing or ostracizing their partner, they needed to let all of these feelings go and continue to support each other completely. Since that marathon day, he was less arrogant and more of a team player. The four of them continued to run in the mornings after work, several times a week. I was so impressed. There could have been winners and losers in that group, but they all came out of the race as winners.

I asked Bob if he was going to run the L.A. Marathon next year. I was already looking forward to beginning training in the fall. He said, "No. I never, ever want to run another marathon." I had hoped that after completing the event, he would find the joy in it, but he was adamant in his decision.

I was disappointed. I wanted him to love it, and he and his partners had such a successful marathon. I just couldn't understand why there wasn't something positive in his experience. Finally, I asked if there wasn't something, anything, he had gleaned from this. He smiled a little and then sat back in his chair to tell me this story.

After the marathon, they were back at work. They were trying to stop some drug deals that had been occurring in a public park. The park was big, and they hadn't been successful in pin pointing where the deals were taking place. One night, they decided on two places, where there had been reports of locations that were good possibilities of something happening. Two of the partners were in a car near one spot. Bob and the fourth partner were in the van at the other location. The drug deal happened in Bob's area. He and his partner jumped out of the van. His partner yelled, "I'll take the buyer." He took off and had the middle aged, couch potato down in minutes.

Bob went after the dealer. He was young and very fit. He was ahead of Bob and getting away, but Bob just kept running, not at all concerned. After all, he had just finished a marathon. Maybe he wasn't as fast as the dealer, but he was certain he could go longer. He caught up with the guy, tackled him and cuffed him. When Bob turned him over, the younger man looked at Bob and was so surprised. "Why, you're an old man." he said, in disbelief.

We all laughed, and Bob said, "No, Jerry. I don't want to run another marathon." This time I was fine with his answer. He definitely won this one.

Acrostic: Procrastinate

BY ELLEN ESTILAI

Pave away! Ignore the slippery road's good intentions.

Read the prompt. Read it again. Over and over.

Overthink it.

Cringe into a rabbit hole and binge-watch childhood memories.

Rotate your tires and spin your wheels.

Ask Alexa for a writing prompt.

(She will say, "Welcome to the Self-Publishing School of Writing Prompts. Write out seven ways you can practice self-care and why this is important to you.")

Then take care of yourself. Eliminate all screen time, especially blank white screens.

Imagine you will never write again.

Name names. Forgive but never forget—or not.

Amend every fourth line of everything you've ever written.

Talk about writing, read about writing, then do all the other things—do

Everything but write.

Saffron Prayers

BY ELLEN ESTILAI

Do not forget our pen cutter, frail *ghalambor*.
Who severed the reed from its bed? Hail, *ghalambor*!

Rumi's reed flute cries out, longs for its marshy home.
Pen, like flute, bereft—an orphan's wail: *Ghalamboooor*!.

Knife scrapes away bark, bevels to acuity,
abrades tender core—his hands can't fail, *ghalambor*.

Others will guide his pens, stream swirls and wisps of ink.
Scribes ignore their agents and prevail, ghalambor.

Inks dark as the reed bed's loam obscure the parent
of their pens, obliterate, assail Ghalambor.

Do you cry out, ache for reunion with your pens,
long to write your story of travail, Ghalambor?

This manner of melancholy calls for saffron,
honey-sweet saltiness to restore pale Ghalambor.

Dip your pen in liquid saffron, write your prayers,
steep them in water orange as sunset's veil, Ghalambor.

Drink sunset water laced with prayers for lost reeds,
prayers for you, that we hear your tale, Ghalambor.

Let Ellen, deep in inky doubt, steep saffron prayers,
that of your lost pen she may avail, Ghalambor.

[Note: This poem is based on my essay of the same name that
appeared in *Writing from Inlandia 2016* and in the online journal
Riddled with Arrows, November 2018.]

Cans at the Curb

BY NAN FRIEDLEY

overfilled with flattened
Amazon boxes, wrapping paper
remnants, limp mylar balloons droop
from the lid of my neighbor's blue
recycle bin across the street, leavings
of their toddler's birthday party

next door neighbor Jeff, hired
a tree trimmer for his giant palm
tree by the fence. Palm fronds
like huge fans poke
from the lid of his green
yard waste container

my brown bin is nearly
empty with a few leftover
bones from BBQ ribs, cantaloupe
rind, wilted lettuce leaves
pungent scent wafting
up the street powered by
an early morning breeze
on my quiet cul-de-sac

Cluck

by Nan Friedley

Tiny gentle woman, she
Kept a daily diary, recorded
Events to recall later, fearing
her memory was fading

On this hot summer day
She donned yellow rubber gloves
Sensible low-heeled shoes
Well-worn bib apron, garb

She saved for the slaughter
Plucked one from the henhouse
Held it by its hocks, laid
It on a concrete block, stomped

On its scrawny neck, wrenched
Off its head with a twist, decapitated
Its wings flapped its body flopped
Metallic scent of blood

Feathers plucked, innards out
Wings, thighs, breasts
Wrapped in freezer paper
Waiting to be a Sunday dinner

Today's diary entry
"Busy day butchering chickens"

The Piano Tuner

BY NAN FRIEDLEY

with his metal tool box in hand
he seats himself on the bench
carefully removes the cabinet door
to expose the strings of our
used blonde Kimball upright

I watch him as he unwraps his
meager tools…tuning hammer
felt strips and the gift of perfect pitch
starting with what I think are
the two strings of middle C
he wraps them in felt to stay
separate as he taps the key, C,C,C,C
C,C,C,C, tightens the pins to tune

he continues the process
of this first octave, then the next
and the next until all two hundred thirty
strings and seven octaves are
in sync, a tedious task, then checks his
work by playing a medley of 40s tunes
that he performs every Saturday at the local
American Legion with the Rex Steffy Trio
for couples swaying on the dance floor

♫ Paper Doll ♫
♫ Stardust ♫
♫ Moonlight Serenade ♫

Waiting Room

BY NAN FRIEDLEY

patient maskers crowd together
as we wait on stiff, straight-back
chairs with armrests of metal on a
busy Thursday morning
after canceled appointments
during the holidays

as I scan the crowd, I wonder what is
hidden under sleeves, pant legs, zippers
red itchy rashes, scaly plaques, cancerous
moles or Dr. Pimple Popper jumbo cysts
we all have something

I brought a book to read, a retired
marine in a cap shares Ben Shapiro's
right-wing podcast on his speakerphone
chatty guy with crutches loudly reminds
check- in staff he's been waiting 45 minutes

after my 30 minute wait I'm called
to an exam room for a quick perusal
of my skin, chat with the doc, an order
for blood work brings me a step closer to a lab
with a different waiting room

Between the Sun and Moon

by Fred García

In the shadow of our own reflection
I find solace in your warm embrace

    I find solace in your warm embrace
    Submerged and scorched in molten earth

Surrendered to the scorch of Earth
Adobe bricks break back into dust

    My adobe stone walls become dust
    Our Mother sighs a breath of relief

Our Mother breathes life as well as relief
Suffering is the only guarantee

    Suffering is the only guarantee
    A life to remember is twice lived

Life worth remembering is lived twice
In the shadow of our own reflection

Vast Wonder

BY FRED GARCÍA

When I was little I
would stare at the pale blue sky
while my mother recalled pig-tailed memories of
endless curiosity creviced in runaway clouds.

And in the night sky we'd find
the moon, Her soft face washed on ours with
thoughts of Grandfather, the farmer, planting seeds–
gaze fixed on Her phases.

Cosmic mysteries, our only inheritance; I
breathe in the sparse constellation
of skywatchers, dreamers
in the dark, searching for
stories in the stars.

My Adopted Country

BY RAGINI GOEL

Lady Liberty opened its gate,
On 27th December, 1968
I came here on that magic date
From the warm climate of India
To the snowy United States!

Everything seemed so cold and dreary,
Strange and lonely, desolate
T'was the sixties and yet
I didn't feel groovy,
I didn't feel great!

Missed my family
Missed my friends
Found a corner to gravitate
"'Leave me alone'" I said
I just want to vegetate

Stepped out of my corner
And said this is no fun,
Let's try and integrate
Staying aloof is real boring,
I would like to assimilate!

So I joined the
Human Relations Commission
which taught me to love and not to hate

Not to prejudge and stereotype
and never, ever to discriminate!

I think back, I ponder
On the last several years
And as I contemplate,
All said and done
My adopted country is great!

Ukraine War Sonnet

BY MARK GRINYER

Comrade Vlad, what's happening with those boys
    in tanks and trucks and rocket launchers sent
    through old Ukrainian streets, in expensive toys
    pursuing your lost memories, angst long pent

In twisted tangles, the wreckage of your lost soul
    homeless outside the garden of dead Red dreams
    rotting in the compost of history's on-line troll
    no more than muddled memories, old memes

Remembered in your heart, I'm sure, as times
    of glory, dragged from suffering years of war
    starvation defeating Nazi invasions, crimes,
    the Holocaust brought on by capitalists of yore,

Remembered now in these your violent choices,
    condemned as hateful by new-world-order voices.

It's Too Damned Cold Outside

by Mark Grinyer

To sit on a porch and watch the rain
as it drizzles some drought away—
the recent past when for months after
years the dry days passed without
a drop or stain to make the high blue
skies turn gray—entrain the chill
of an arctic reach down south to soak
our southwest desert landscape in
the green of growing things the lift
of wings, where acres of wildflowers
break the ground and raise new colors
for all to see and celebrate, despite
the crunch of burnt-off brush and ashen
dust in flooding streets and canyon floors
that carry all this cold wet weather down
to coastal plains and seaside towns
where people beach like dead white whales
in flood tides raised by our neglect—
the silent years through which we failed
to act or change the ways we face the earth
and deal with all the complex turns
of living worlds, where arid land awaits
the winter storm's return and we regret
the cold wet days on which we curse
the rain—resent the flowing water's rush
or lose ourselves in Pacific reaches
empty of all those souls who choose
to make these lands their home
away from pain where they can sit
on a cold back porch and watch
the flooding rainfall write
some wordless drought away.

Thanksgiving, 2022

BY MARK GRINYER

Dark-eyed juncos jink and hop
from wall to branch to fence and up
to the empty feeder above my yard.
I watch them search.

Thanksgiving day may have come
but inflations's up and we cannot
afford another big bag of seed
to feed them with today.

They must find less easy fare
to fill their crops and keep them warm
on this winter stop in their annual flight
from northwest rain to southwest drought.

The Morning Opens

by Mark Grinyer

With the first cold breath as I step outside
to the sound of wind in trees out back
The morning opens like an unwritten page
or the taste and smell of my first hot cup
of espresso brewed before breakfast light.

Oregon juncos, and white-crowned sparrows
chirp and flit in the morning shade
feathers fluffed to fight the chill
of early winter's shrinking days
the start of festive seasons of praise.

They model my future in the opening light
the shortened days, memories of night in
the encroaching chill of an aging year
that awakens me in the dark before dawn
with the season's rapturous songbird jeer.

Jacaranda

BY MARK GRINYER

Jacaranda petals
scattered on the ground

Some glowing purple
some gone gray-brown

A two-colored ramble
on concrete or clay

Mortality's symbol
or the end of a day

Just Me

by Carmen Melendez-Gutierrez

I was born in a little town in the middle of the island of Puerto Rico. I came to this world with the help of a midwife (comadrona), madrina Castula. It was a hot summer day, as told by my family members. I was the middle child of five siblings, two older brothers, a younger brother, and a younger sister. Growing up around my grandparents and cousins, life was tough but we were happy. Life was simple. For the first 7 years of my life I was raised in the neighborhood of La Loma (el barrio). I lived in a few houses from my grandparents: Papá Juan and Mamá Ramona. Ramona Marquez was my grandmother. She was very special and fundamental in my upbringing, unfortunately she died young. She died on October 12, 1969. About my father, I can't find it in my heart to love him or forgive him for all the suffering he causes my family. I mean my mother died when she was 52, I always think that indirectly he killed her "a cuchillo de palo". I do not remember any happy moments with my father. He never was a father, supported us or gave us advice, on the contrary he was an abusive father and husband. He even stole from us. My mother was the first wife, when my mother was pregnant with me, he got another woman, who had a daughter months after I was born, and guess what, he named her second daughter Carmen, just like my mother and me. He named my half sister from another mother after my mother to make her feel better for having a "corteja", so he said. That tells you how ignorant he was.

When I was 7 we moved to town, to the projects (el caserío). The people in my hometown were friendly and kind. I remember living in the "caserío" and seeing a whole new world compared to living in a farm-like atmosphere. I got tough by necessity. Walking home from school occasionally encounters a bully named Nora.

My joy was to visit my maternal grandmother in Pinas, another community in my hometown where my mother grew up. I remember the hacienda 'Las Posas", my maternal grandparents' home. It was remote and as progress showed they built a house by the main road, but my grandfather Pablo and his two brothers: Visitación (Becho) and Tio Jacinto continue working the hacienda. I will go with my uncle Jose Manuel to bring "fiambreras" with lunch to them. On the way there we go near the "cascadas" and play with the water. I love it that every Sunday all the family will gather for a meal. It was the best memories playing with my cousins.

In 1969, I was 15-years-old when my dear grandma, Mamá Ramona died. I remember Titi Narcisa traveled from New York for the funeral. She was so beautiful and bitchy. Later I learned she was a pin up girl and a singer in the 60's. She married some Aguilar guy from Mexico, who was later famous. Titi Narcisa died in a fire in New Jersey with 6 or 7 of his grandkids. That was such a tragedy for the whole family. I remember titi Lydia went to New Jersey for the funerals and brought many newspapers with articles of this awful event.

I graduated in 1972 from high school and went to graduate school for 6 months to study drafting but had to stop due to financial hardship. I really wanted to study Pharmacy but was unable to get into the university again due to financial hardship. I asked my dad to use his military benefits to sponsor my studies and he refused. Later, I went to a vocational school and studied Banking Service, and started working for Banco Popular de Puerto Rico, a major financial institution on the island. I worked for Banco Popular for 3 years, 1974-1977. I started in Hato Rey, La Milla de Oro. I worked at the vault (La Boveda), with Mr. Ruiz-Chaar, and Mayito. I have the best memories of those years. A lot of good stuff happened to me. I met Jaime and Papo. I also worked as a "relief" teller for the Metropolitan Area, visiting 26 different branches. I was working at LD, (Loan Department) in

Cupey Center when I met Papo. He was the love of my life. I also met Gerardo, Papo's best friend. I was fired from this job because I was always late. I was late for work almost every day, but this was not my choice. No matter how early I woke up trying to win time, I was traveling from Comerio to San Juan and the transportation was awful. I was good at what I was doing. I got many achievements and was praised constantly by all customers, co-workers, and superiors.

During this time I was able to buy a house in Bayamon for my mother. My oldest brother Junior and his wife Milagros lived there with us. Unfortunately we lost that house. I was the only one working and "no pude con la carga"

In 1979 I joined the PR National Guard and went to training in Fort Benjamin Harrison, Indiana, where I met my husband who I married in 1980. Meeting Pedro was a "love story". After I finished a class at the Administration Building in Fort Benjamin Harrison in Indiana, I was walking down the stairs when I saw this guy that mesmerized me. I was attending Finance training for the PR National Guard. He was walking up the stairs, me, down, our eyes met and continued looking at each other for a while. Cupid did his duty! We did not speak a word. He was hot! Eric Estrada look alike! Later I learned he was also Puerto Rican. I continued walking to my room, there I started telling my room-mate Rita how I just met the guy I was going to marry! She laughed at me, made fun of me and told me "you are so roman-tic". Days passed and I saw this guy at the mess hall (at this point I still had not talked to him). He looked at me, I looked at him, another spark! This time he smiled at me and I froze. I felt stupid. Weeks later Rita had a date and hooked me up with her date's best friend. Rita's date happens to be the guy I met walking down the stairs. I ended up being with that guy and Rita was so mad at me. Years later I married this guy.

March is a special month for me. I left Puerto Rico on March

18 of 1980. Got married on the 22nd of March, 3 days after I arrived in California. I was supposed to visit and stay with my friend Shelly during my vacations but never made it to her place. Instead she took Pedro with her to the airport to pick me up. It was a surprise for me! Pedro received me with the most beautiful red roses arrangement. He took me to dinner at a very nice Chinese food restaurant in the Hollywood Hills, then to his apartment where I had the most amazing experience. I fell in love with the guy all over again. I went back to Puerto Rico to quit my job and to pick my favorite things to move to California. I remember the day I said goodbye to my mom. The radio was playing Michael Jackson's "Rock With Me". I lived with Pedro in his apartment in Covina, CA for a little while and then we rented a really nice place in Rowland Heights, CA.

I got pregnant but lost my first baby. I was unhappy that I left my sick mother behind, I think that had to do a lot for my miscarriage. I left PR because I was so tired of being responsible for being the only one taking care of my mother. My two older brothers did nothing, my two younger siblings did less. So I left far, far away to California. That same year I had to go back because my mother got pneumonia. She died while I was there and stayed for her funeral. She was 52 when she died. That caused me such trauma that when I reached 52, (and because every time I went to Puerto Rico people in my family commented on how much I looked like my mother), I thought I was going to die. In that year, 2006, I traveled, on my own, in my little Toyota Corolla car, from California to Florida. I called it the "menopausal rampage"

I had my first child Gloriani in 1982, she was born in the Army military base of Fort Ord, California. From there we moved to Hawaii where my second daughter Monica was born in Tripler Army Hospital. We were living in the Army base Fort Shafter. While living in this house on Macomb Dr, my sister Annie and nephew Felix came to visit in Hawaii.

After I left my husband, I left Hawaii and went to live in Riverside, California with my two daughters, my sister and my nephew. Every night we watched a soap opera called "CRYSTAL". One time they announced that the characters of "Crystal" would be in Riverside at the now known as the Fox Theater. I always wanted to be a reporter so the night of the show, me and my sister dressed up really fancy and went to the theater pretending to be reporters. They never asked us for any identification, we had a camera and for some unknown reason they let us go in and mingle with the stars. I took pictures with me and each and everyone of the stars. I still remember the thrill!

2000 was a special year. I went to Puerto Rico for my class reunion, re-encountered an old friend and had a passionate 2 weeks affair, then came back home to California.

All my life I LOVE making movies but 2001 - 2002 was my peak! I made a few movies, and met some celebrities. I still dream about making THE ONE.

2018 seems to be the year!

Being a single mother was not easy. I struggled to communicate with my family with the best words I could so they wouldn't take it the wrong way. It makes me so mad that my kids did not respect me. I felt that as a mom I was not strict, firm or strong enough to stand up and discipline my kids.

In my family the oldest living is my brother Junior, but he is in Puerto Rico, but in California I am the queen! I am the oldest Melendez in California. In Puerto Rico I have the most amazing group of friends in my hometown, my classmates. Even after more than 49 years when I graduated from high school, I still keep in touch with my childhood friends.

I am so proud of myself and my sister. We came to this country as "jíbaritas" and we survived. We raised our kids by ourselves. We were able to create many achievements. Today my heart is broken because 2 years ago my sister died suddenly. No one expected it.

One Sunday we were having lunch and going shopping and the next morning she died of a heart attack. I often wonder what would have been if I would have stayed in Puerto Rico, but this is the path that God chose for me. I miss my island, but my loved ones are here. Would I ever go back to live there?

Awake

BY MILAN HAMILTON

Staying awake is
Akin to being alive—
Even if to be awoke
By a train horn
Testing our senses
Calling to attention
For one last hurrah!

There was a Queen
She stayed awake
Almost a century.
Was she watching
All unfolding
Like a Mona Lisa,
Enigmatically?

There was a guy
Slept through it all—
When he awoke
He found it strange
To hear the sounds
To smell the fragrant
Flowers on his grave.

I'd rather be awake
And walk the earth
With friends of many kinds;
Mostly the vulnerable
Like Holden Caulfield
As the Catcher in the Rye,
Watchfully.

Complete

(a Villanelle)

BY MILAN HAMILTON

Let me not try to rewrite the whole;
I'm in too deep, the story is mine.
The die is cast, the dice are rolled.

There'll never be for one so old
A chance to redo a minute of time
Let me not try to rewrite the whole.

Enough! I say, and were I so bold
To venture a crossing of that line
The die is cast, the dice are rolled.

Yet there is that thought that some would hold
That seeks an answer that none can find—
Let me not try to rewrite the whole.

And as the bird I saw this morning told
Me: "Think you the past can be refined?
The die is cast, the dice are rolled."

No at eighty-five my cup is full,
My life still to be complete, like aging wine.
Let me not try to rewrite the whole
The die is cast, the dice are rolled.

I Shall Not Die Alone

BY MILAN HAMILTON

I shall not die alone
Should I be the last on earth
Of my kind, for I saw
Blossoming, on my walk today,
A thousand yellow daisies
Arrayed for my viewing, alone,
As I took my morning stroll
To Starbucks.

I shall not die alone
For I have lived to see
Ten thousand sunsets, and
As many risings
To feel the warmth of his rays
On my face.

I shall not die alone
For I have known the tender touch
Of a woman, and the cold nose
Of a dog, quivering with delight
At my return, and the soft purr
Of a cat nestled against my back
As I slept.

All these are with me, and not
Only these, in every moment
Of solitude
And will be as my last breath
Is taken.

The Poetry Curse

by Milan Hamilton

I'm cursed with the poetry curse
I find myself writing in lines
Whether couplets or quatrains
Sometimes in blank verse.

Sometimes they rhyme
I'm surprised when they do
My brain now refuses
To lapse into prose
My pen seems to follow
Strange, mysterious urges
Possessed by the gods
Or the demons perhaps.

I've given up trying
To figure it out
I've come to conclude that
For better or worse
I'll forever be under
The Poetry Curse.

Awesome View

BY MILAN HAMILTON

At fifty-three, and halfway up El Capitan's three-thousand-foot sheer granite face, he wondered if he had the strength, the endurance, to reach the summit. This was no time to start letting those kinds of thoughts take hold. He had seen the documentary *Free Solo* more than once. Alex Honnold in 2017 had reached the summit, which usually takes several days and tons of equipment, in less than four hours. And with only his hands and feet to propel him upwards. And here was another Alex, Alexander Hamilton (distant relation), experienced climber who should have nothing more to prove, harness, device, carabiner, climbing rope and cam, and lots of pitons for security, heading up the treacherous "freerider route," hesitantly but resolutely. Until now.

His career began running like a movie in a series of fast-forward clips, one after another. He had made attempts at the summits of Anapurna and Everest in the Himalayas, the famous Matterhorn of Switzerland, Mt. Dinali in Alaska, some of the most formidable and deadly ascents. He had never been a free solo rock climber before, except for some of the popular touristy destinations in the U.S., Joshua Tree in California, Zion in Utah, and the Devil's Tower in Wyoming. El Capitan has always been considered one of the most brutal climbing challenges anywhere in the world. So maybe he was trying to prove something, he wasn't sure what or to whom. But here he was, plastered against this hard flat surface, calloused fingers gripping cracks and toes flexing to keep him from dangling. "OK, enough thinking, fifteen-hundred feet, or miles, to go! No matter, onward and upward!"

Suddenly there was this pinging sound, then another, then a third. "Oh damn, I thought I'd pounded those pitons in securely. If any more go, I am in trouble. That rope is going to be swinging loose and so am I." The dreaded ping came like the final gong of his meditation bell as he was jarred into awareness of his mortality.

Flattening himself against the cold rock face of El Capitan, he turned his face as far in both directions as his neck would stretch and heard himself shout: "God, what an awesome view!"

What Lies Beneath

BY EDNA HELED

For an entire week the bay out my window was buzzing: kayaks, surf boards, sea motorbikes, herds of binocular-armoured exposed-bellied know-it-all chaps and their exhilarated wives. I watched them going up and down the tide, pointing to the sea, making big gestures, boasting. Spotting became as triumphal as winning a medal in extreme sport.

I didn't get to see her, but it seems that I was the only one. 'Whale and Dolphin Watch" was bombarded with photos shot from neighbouring houses on my street, featuring the magnetic creature circling the cove's waters. My eyes popped to spot a spout of white foam in the blue vastness, a jet of joyous sprinkle, a whiff from the mystery of the underwater.

How elated we feel when we get a message from the deep. A few glimpses of a tail or a fin are jolts of wonder, access to the realm of Gods. After a few days, I realised that the mere thought of a whale dancing right outside my window was enough to thrill me. Knowing she was there in the viewing range, that maybe tomorrow I'll get lucky, was all I needed to connect me to the admirable force of nature.

And then, I did see her. A whale indeed, a special whale, a Gray's Beaked whale. "Rare to find such a specimen of deep-water species in the shallows," reported DOC.

I saw her. She had clear shark bite marks over her body.

She was washed to the beach at dusk.

She Fooled Me Again

BY RICHARD HESS

This is a story about me and my 2 children. At the time of this story my daughter Carrie was 9 and my son Brian was 7. Brian was recovering from a viral illness – slight fever, nausea, generally not feeling well. He had missed school for 3 days. But now he was over it. He was running around, happy, full of energy.

Then Carrie said, "Dad, I will make you a bet that Brian stays home from school tomorrow. 10 bucks." I took this bet because I thought there was no way I could lose. Brian looked perfectly healthy. Obviously, I would not take her money, just have the great satisfaction of winning the bet. Because even at age 9 my daughter had a remarkable ability to trick me and fool me.

Well, the next morning I came into the living room. Brian was there and he looked great!! I thought "Surely he is going to school today." Then Carrie came in and spoke in a very concerned voice. "Brian how do you feel? You look really pale. Is your tummy upset? Do you feel like you might throw up? Are your muscles weak and achy? Let me check your forehead. Oh, you feel hot. I think you might have a fever!" You should go sit down and rest. Carrie then told Mom, "Brian is not feeling well. He is sick. I think he needs to stay home from school today." Mom asked Brian how he felt, and he said he felt kinda weak and sick. Mom decided he should stay home. I protested this decision citing the lack of a demonstrated fever, i.e. temperature of 100.4 degrees or higher. But this was to no avail. In such matters Mom's decision is final. Bottom line – Brian stayed home from school, Carrie won the bet and my 10 dollars. And Brian was happy because he really didn't want to go to school anyway. The only loser was me.

This made me realize that this is what we often do to ourselves. We get up in the morning and think," I'm tired, I didn't sleep well. I have no energy. I look in the mirror and see my tired, bloodshot eyes. I think, "When I feel like this, I usually get a headache – yes, there is one starting. And usually my back starts hurting – ok I feel that sacroiliac pain now. Surely, I will have a lousy day. Everyone will be difficult and annoying. So, my whole day will be a nightmare – and probably the rest of the week as well.

Well, what should we do? If we have a pain – ok we do, but don't generalize to everything else. Don't exaggerate or 'catastrophize'. Counter negative thoughts with positive ones which are more accurate about what is really going on.

Be thankful for what you do have. I am alive and most body parts are still working – kindof. And the pain is minimal, especially if I think about something positive, like my amazing beautiful 19-month-old granddaughters. Life is good!

Thanksgiving

BY RICHARD HESS

Ah, Thanksgiving! I think back to my childhood. Our family would meet in Philadelphia at the home of my dear Aunt Goldie, a registered nurse with a ribald sense of humor. True, Thanksgiving is a day of family and turkey, yeah, all of that. But, more importantly, in my mind, it is a day of football. I would of course be watching the game while the ladies were cooking in the kitchen. Typically, for 3 quarters, the game is not very exciting. The teams go back and forth, mainly kicking field goals. Finally, in the fourth quarter, the game gets very interesting. Time is running out. The Packers are moving down the field. If they can score a touchdown, they win the game. Wow, this is so exciting! Then that dreaded call comes from the dining room. "The food is ready – come now!" Oh, crap! Why does this always happen at the worst time? Maybe I can stall. Make believe I didn't hear them. Although they did yell pretty loud. One more critical play and – Oh, no! The Packers called time out! So, I go to the dining room for the turkey and return to hear the announcer tell how this was such a terrific game, truly an epic. Oh well, better luck next year, Richie.

And this bad football luck did not end there. When I was the OB doc on call at the hospital, it was déjà vu all over again, to quote Yogi Berra. You cannot believe how many babies are born in the fourth quarter of really good football games. So, here I am, waiting in the doctors' call room, watching the game. These 2 teams are fighting for a chance to go to the Superbowl. It is the fourth quarter and time is running out. The losing team is marching down the field. A score would win the game for them.

Then the phone rings. "216 is pushing, getting ready to deliver. "What? She has to push now. Why now for heaven's sake?" I thought to myself. The nurse is aware that I am watching the football game and knows she must take a sterner tone. "Yes, you must come NOW." I know that tomorrow my partner, Lawrie Dunlap, will tell me how this was the best game he has ever watched, and I can only muster a feeble smile.

But I was not alone. This sports fascination also affected many expectant fathers. Now expectant fathers are usually present in the birthing rooms.

The birthing rooms also had TVs. Often the husband would sit at the foot of the bed watching a game on the far wall. Ice hockey was very popular in Fairbanks. Many guys would watch these games on TV, paying little or no attention to their wives. Instead of helping their wives, they would be fixated on the TV. The Mom-to-be would loudly exclaim "Herman, I'm having a contraction!" The husband, clearly more focused on the hockey game than his wife's labor, would reply, "That's nice dear. Wow, did you see that goal?" The nurse would nicely remind the Dad that he should be with his wife, showing her love and encouragement. The Dad would say, "Okay, I'm coming", then linger for a few more seconds to watch for the goal that he was sure was imminent. Finally, he would come to his wife. Then the nurse would remotely turn off the TV and he would give an audible sigh.

I feel your pain, brother. I really do.

Grandma's Treasure Box

BY CONNIE JAMESON

Grandma's treasure box, what's inside?
Grandma's treasure box, what will we find?

What did she hold so near and dear?
What did she keep year after year?

In Grandma's treasure box, soon we'll know
For Grandma's treasure box, it will show

What brought her joy, a smile to her face
Precious memories time could not erase

Cards we'd signed with childish scrawl
Crayon drawings she'd hang upon her wall

Our photographs, edges curled with age
Letters we wrote, she saved every page

Those silly trinkets that we'd bring
A pretty little stone, a dime-store ring

Little things given from the heart
So, from them, she would never part

Nothing of value to others' eyes
But for her, brought happy sighs

Grandma's treasure box, now we know
How our Grandma loved us so!

Growing Up

BY CONNIE JAMESON

Growing up is not always easy
Life can be rough and tough
Sometimes your parents' efforts
Are just not quite enough

That's when another person
Can lend an ear or give a hand
Making all the difference
To help you understand

Just knowing someone's there
Who really cares for you
Accepts you with your problems
Helps you know what to do

That very special someone
So sincere and real
When they say "It'll be okay"
And "I care how you feel"

Someone that you know
You can trust and rely on
Always ready to provide
A shoulder you can cry on

Someone to pat your back
Say "I know that you're trying"
You need not feel ashamed
If they should see you crying

Someone who will provide
That much needed suggestion
The one that finally points you
In the right direction

That someone might be
A scout leader, a coach, a teacher
Or maybe a neighbor
A relative, a preacher

Are YOU that someone?

Grandpa

BY CONNIE JAMESON

Don't leave me, Grandpa
What will I do without you?
I'll miss you so

His body is still, so still
I study his chest
It rises and falls, but barely

I take his hand and place it gently in mine
Noting the details—lines, veins, age spots
Thinking of all these hands have done in his long life

They say it won't be long now
Someone said his body is like
A flickering candlelight in the wind
Soon to be extinguished

This makes me start to cry
And I have this crazy thought
Could it be my tears that put out
That last little flickering flame
Of my grandpa's life?

Grandpa, I don't want you to go
But, what do *you* want?
Do you wish for that little wind to finally bring
A dark, calm, peaceful end?

No matter when that end comes, Grandpa
You'll continue to be a candlelight for me
Your loving memory will always help light my way
I love you, Grandpa

"It was a fight or flight moment and I sprouted wings"

BY CONNIE JAMESON

It was a fight or flight moment and I sprouted wings
I sprouted wings again
Again and again and again
As I always seem to do

Instead of standing up
Instead of speaking up
I'm just up, up, up
And away from the situation
But these wings don't help me soar
No, just escape

I don't say what should be said
Nor do what should be done
I don't state my views
I don't fight for my cause
I just close my lips and swallow my voice

I experience no exhilaration of resolve
Just the disappointment of resignation

If I continue to sprout wings
Every time there is conflict
I'll eventually feel the weight of wings
Unable to fight or take flight
But just give up
Cease to care
Be nothing
Lying there
Hidden under all those wings

Love at First Sight

BY CONNIE JAMESON

It was "love at first sight"
That delectable delight displayed on the dessert cart

Resting on a flaky, melt-in-your-mouth crust
A lovely layer of lemon cream
Teasing my tastebuds with thoughts of its tantalizing, tangy, tart taste

Atop the luscious-looking lemon layer
A fluffy mound of whipped cream
Little rivulets of dark chocolate syrup cascading down its sides
Curls of dark chocolate shavings scattered about
Plump, red raspberries arranged around the base
Completed this masterpiece

Ah! This lovely creation
Piled high with my very favorite flavors
Lemon, raspberry, whipped cream and dark chocolate
But, also loaded with . . . calories!

So, dear waitress, I cannot indulge in this temptation
No, I must instead choose the sugar-free jello
But, please, let me gaze just a little longer
At that special dessert I really crave
The one that was truly "love at first sight"

Reflections on Walking Rubidoux/ Pachappa

BY ANN KANTER

I grew up on a one-block street below what we knew as Mt. Rubidoux in the late 1950's, in the semi-desert of inland Southern California. Our street was named for Isabella, the wife of Frank Miller who built the Mission Inn hotel. The hotel was fashionable in the early 20th century when people would arrive by train and sometimes spend several months at the Mission Inn. A favorite outing for the Mission Inn guests was to motor up Mt. Rubidoux.

By third grade I was regularly scrambling up the mountain with neighbor kids. We climbed on sand-colored boulders, watched small lizards and crouched down to see ant colonies in the silty soil that looked like flour. It was finer than sand and soft to land on if you happened to slide and fall in one of the gullies between switchbacks. Beneath the silt layer is a brown soil that carries the mountain's probable original name, Pachappa. The story goes that Juan Bandini, in the map he submitted with his application for a Mexican land grant, re-named it Mt. Rubidoux. He then called a smaller hill to the south Pachappa, thus greatly increasing the size of his ranch.

Near the beginning of the mile and half walk up Rubidoux/ Pachappa there is a triangle with large boulders and plaques dedicated to Father Junipero Serra, founder of the California missions, and to Henry Huntington, one of the California railroad and real estate barons. Huntington bought the mountain in 1906 and gave it to his friend Frank Miller of the Mission Inn, and it was later granted to the City of Riverside as parkland. A controversy continues to simmer about the placing of a large cross on top of the mountain, and eventually a private foundation bought the land surrounding the cross so that it would not be on City property.

For thousands of years, the Tongva tribe lived along the river below, and the mountain was sacred to them. But the Spanish relocated the Tongva to the San Gabriel Mission. While their villages did not survive, Tongva tribal members today are sharing the deep taproot of their history, which is critical to understanding what we now call Mt. Rubidoux and the Santa Ana River Valley below it.

Continuing up the mountain you come to the Peace Tower and Bridge, built by Frank Miller in the Mission style. Miller was an advocate of peace missions and an avid collector of Asian art, especially bells. However, there was a strong "white California" movement in the early 20th century, and the State Legislature was debating whether to permanently segregate public schools. This was a source of embarrassment to President Woodrow Wilson, especially after Japan had fought on the side of the U.S. in World War I and participated in the Treaty of Versailles. The school segregation plan was dropped, but in return the Japanese Government agreed to severely restrict the number of brides permitted to leave Japan. Within a few more years, U.S. immigration laws almost completely eliminated immigration from non-European countries in the draconian 1924 immigration bill. Miller's response to all of this was to build living quarters for the Japanese and Chinese laborers who could not own land in California, but who worked at the Mission Inn year-round. And shortly after a trip to Japan, Miller built his Peace Bridge in 1925, concretely expressing his vision of a California that would be open to the world.

From the Peace Bridge you can look north to a lower hill where Miller was the producer of the first Christian nondenominational Easter Sunrise Service in April 1909. This event became immensely popular and by 1915 the SP railroad had put on a special trolley run from Los Angeles. By the 1920's, the Riverside Easter Sunrise service had a peak attendance of 30,000, the largest in the country where many other communities had also adopted the tradition.

The opera singer Marcella Craft gave a famous performance for the Easter Sunrise Service in 1915. She sang "The Holy City," one of the most popular and pirated pieces of sheet music of the time. Today this vision of the "New Jerusalem" is easily viewable on Youtube. Marcella had grown up in Riverside. In her childhood, Riverside was a small town built on a dry plateau ringed by the transverse mountain range. Since Spanish times it had been used as grazing land for cattle, sheep and horses. In the late 1870's, canals were built and the place was transformed into orange groves, resulting in the second, and most lucrative, gold rush to California. Victoria Avenue was built by English gentlemen farmers. Many of the growers wanted to import European "high" culture, and Marcella (then Marcia) studied singing. Frank Miller appreciated her talent and sent her to Boston with her mother, where she sang for two years for Mary Baker Eddy at the Mother Temple for Christian Science. Miller supported further studies for her in Italy, and she had an important career in Germany, performing Madame Butterfly with Caruso in Munich, until she retired and returned to Riverside early in the 1930's.

I encountered Marcella many years later in the early 1960's, after she had formed the Riverside Opera Company, where my ballet class performed at Memorial Auditorium. (During La Traviata I accidentally kicked a member of the chorus, an older woman in a gypsy costume. I was sorry but Marcella had warned the chorus not to crowd in too close around us dancers.) Marcella had unnaturally dyed brown hair, a cane, and she impatiently mediated conflicts between the soloists, whom she recruited from out of town, and the chorus who were amateur Riversiders. The chorus included my mother and aunt who later sang in Madame Butterfly wearing black wigs.

Last year I decided to look up the Riverside Easter Sunrise Service on Youtube. I had never actually seen the service as a child, only listened to the early morning singing that came through my window. But since the Youtube video was made in

2021 during COVID, there was almost no one in attendance, only a country western band playing hymns before a small group on the hill where Marcella Craft once sang.

My mother, who still lives in our house on Isabella Street, texted me on Easter, attaching an image of an old postcard of Mt. Rubidoux. Model T Fords were lined up back to back, completely filling the road up the mountain and the small plaza beneath the cross. These days that road is filled with hundreds of people of all ages, pushing baby carriages, some walking fast to get their "steps" in, circling the 1331 foot mountain. There are no cars, and there is silence except for the sound of footsteps, hushed fragments of conversation and an occasional radio. The 360-degree views from the top are extraordinary. The mountain somehow remains sacred, a place for listening and remembering. Perhaps this is due to its tenacious plant and animal life, its ancient boulders, and all those who have loved to climb the mountain through the centuries.

A Bride's Thanksgiving
by Margo Klein

Plot

A young bride celebrates her first Thanksgiving as a wife. Her husband is an Army Captain and he commands a Company at Fort Hood, Texas. It is customary for the commanding officer to invite all his junior officers and their families to Thanksgiving Dinner at his quarters. The only problem is that his newly acquired wife doesn't know how to cook. Misadventures are inevitable.

Act 1

Honey, I have some news. We are going to host about 20 people for Thanksgiving. But don't worry, I'll help with the dishes.

Are you insane?? Have you not noticed that I can't cook?

Well, of course I've noticed. But how hard can it be? Didn't you ever help your Mom cook Thanksgiving?

My mom doesn't cook, we go to relatives for Thanksgiving. We always bring those cans of biscuits you whack on the counter as our contribution.

But what did she do the rest of the year if she didn't cook?

She had a system. Mondays we had hotdogs boiled in water. Tuesday we had frozen pot pies. Wednesday's we had canned soup and a sandwich. Thursday was Dinty Moore beef stew, Friday we had fish sticks, Saturday we had TV dinners and Sundays we went to relatives for dinner. Hey, I have an idea. Maybe we can get turkey TV dinners for everyone??

Hmm, no, I really don't think that will work.

Act 2

Thanksgiving is only 2 days away. Young wife has made a plan.

Honey, here's my menu.

Appetizer: Canned fruit cocktail, everyone likes that.

Dinner: Ham (the kind that comes in a can, and you reheat)

Turkey (I'll just put it in the oven with the ham)

Mashed potatoes from a box, Gravy from a can, Biscuits you whack on the counter (an old family recipe), canned green beans, canned cranberry sauce.

Dessert: Frozen Pumpkin Pie and frozen Sara Lee cake.

Husband is not convinced, but he can't cook either! So he gives his approval.

Act 3

Thanksgiving Day

Everyone arrives, most bring alcohol as their contribution, although there is one cheese ball brought by another wife. Show off! Everyone has 3 or 4 drinks before dinner is served. No one cares that the food is mediocre at best. There is a lot of laughter and a few pranks. The young wife learns that there something called giblets wrapped in paper inside the turkey (why would they do that)?? Also basting is not just a sewing term, but something she should have done to her turkey. The day ends happily and young wife decides to take cooking lessons.

Homeless

BY MARGO KLEIN

Homeless
Hopeless
Helpless
Hapless

Bad luck
Bad choices
Bad health
Bad policies
Bad faith

Not enough housing
Not enough clinics
Not enough responsibility
Not enough sympathy
Not enough empathy

It takes a village
It takes money
Not in my backyard
Not my problem

It's a disgrace
Where is their place

Hapless
Helpless
Hopeless
Homeless

A Safe Deposit Box

by Margo Klein

When you want a very safe place to store hard to replace documents and good jewelry, where do you put them? I always thought the answer was a bank safe deposit box. After all, it is inside a bank vault. The walls are made of metal and security is tight. Perfect solution!

My recent experience with Hurricane Ian has shown me that it's not so perfect.

In the days after the hurricane there was no electricity. Nothing was open. The water wasn't safe to drink without boiling. ATMs, gas pumps, traffic lights and dozens of other things don't work without electricity. Life was difficult. We didn't even think about our safe deposit box for a couple of weeks.

After about a week the electricity was restored. When I used the ATM at the bank I could see the bank was still closed but I wasn't worried since about 80% of the businesses were closed. The building was still standing which I took as a good sign. After a couple more weeks the bank (a huge national one) put a trailer in the parking lot to conduct bank business. I'd spent several weeks going through our damaged home, packing up what we could salvage to move, give away or throw out. Now my husband and I were ready to drive across the country and leave hurricane prone Florida behind.

We really needed the stuff in our safe deposit box before we left town. To my horror I was told it would be a long time before anyone would be able to access their boxes. So we had to leave the state without any of our important papers.

Months later we returned to visit relatives for the Holidays . It took many phone calls to find out that access to the boxes was only available on Wednesday mornings between 9-11am by appointment only. A bank officer and a security guard came from another location and escorted you to your box. I was happy to finally be reunited with my jewelry, passport, birth certificate, car title, marriage license etc.

I found out that in a natural disaster, a safe deposit box isn't necessarily safe.

Puma Under the Full Snow Moon

by Joan Koerper (Dr. Mary Joan Koerper)

The full Snow Moon was brilliant against the clear night sky when the Puma came loping around the south side of Robin Circle. She was unmistakable. Graceful. Long sleek body, strong thick full-furred legs, lengthy, and relaxed curved tail. No confusing her for Coyote whose body movements, shape, and size are completely different.

I knew she was in the village of Wrightwood, California, traveling on her own, after raising, and separating from, her cub. She had killed a hundred-pound sheep, about two miles away, within the last ten days. But sightings placed her trekking down canyons east and west of the cabin I live in, or higher up on the San Gabriel Mountain slopes.

Mindful of any number of animals I might encounter in this terrain, at 6,300 feet elevation, I wore my headlamp to augment the moon-lit landscape. My highly-trained, well-socialized, miniature poodle, Gilligan, was snug on his leash in my left hand, while a pointed, metal ski pole was firm in my right. My safety garb for our necessary outings on one-way roads, through towering Jeffrey Pines, sans street lights, after dark. The front yard where I live is not fully fenced.

Less than thirty feet away, Puma followed the road's curve on Robin just before it intersects with, and crosses, Spruce. I was absorbing this breathtaking, sacred, event watching Puma's elegant advance, simultaneously noting that Millie, my friend's and neighbor's dog, was tied up on their porch directly in Puma's path. Standing in the middle of the road where Puma had run a minute earlier, I reached for my phone. We were just fifty feet away from Millie's house, but do you think my phone would ring through quickly?

Millie had spotted Puma and was agitated. I was fairly certain

Puma would continue running east on Robin until… I saw her eyes looking back at us a few feet beyond the side of Millie's house. She'd spun around. Finally, the call went through. Millie was hustled safely inside.

While not turning our back on Puma, Gilligan and I reversed course and casually headed toward our cabin. We had frequently encountered lone coyotes on our walks, but without the pack, they are shy and quickly dart off. Much to my surprise, however, Puma crossed back over Spruce, was once again on Robin Circle, and continued to follow us. We reached the gate to the front yard, which is only fastened to the chain link fence with a bungee cord, stepped inside, and "secured" it.

We turned to Puma and stood our ground looking directly at her. At a distance of forty feet, in the same spot I'd stopped to use the phone, she paused, looked at us, and started to move forward. She could have easily sprinted over the open ground and leapt the five-foot fence. Or, flown through the gate in a flash. But, at no time was I afraid. Neither did Gilligan show any sign of alarm.

"No!" I commanded, and tapped my ski pole twice on a paver. She halted. Then, she started moving forward again. "NO!" I commanded once more and repeated my action. "I can see your eyes. We are looking directly into each other's souls, our eyes… only it looks like I have three eyes because of this headlamp. I want you to live and thrive. I have implored others in the village to learn to live peacefully with you. These are your mountains. Your species is much older than mine, and you have been in these mountains for thousands of years. But, come no closer. We mean you no harm. Go on your way. Blessings."

We stood in motionless silence.

The words of Barry Lopez, one of America's most important nature and wilderness writers, coursed through my veins. He wrote that predators and their prey carry on conversations, an evolutionary dialogue based on stares, scents, gaits, and body movement. The exchange defines the outcome of the hunt. This has certainly been my experience with human and non-human encounters.

We waited, cues given and received, until an unspoken agreement was reached. The energy was clear. All three of us knew we were safe.

Gilligan and I turned and walked down the dirt path to the cabin door.

Safe Harbor

BY JOAN KOERPER (DR. MARY JOAN KOERPER)

waves of sea-driven breezes
evoke deep,
melodious, orchestral tones
from the giant wind chime,
crescendos to momentary rests

Avocado, Elm, and Fern trees
dance in individual,
yet synchronized, movements

gardens overflow:
herbs, vegetables, plants and flowers
carefully tended for over fifty years.
Irresistible olfactory invitations arise
as homemade vegetable pot pies
bake to perfection

calming, strengthening,
flute music wafts
from *Deep Peace*

evacuated. again.
fire rages above
in the San Gabriel Mountains.
cherished Joshua Trees,
Jeffrey Pines, and wildlife
succumb.

Gilligan Dog, Clooney Cat and I
are sheltered, nurtured,
by elemental foundations:
sisterhood, friendship,
love and music.

safe harbors
in the impromptu
composition
of my life.

With deep gratitude to Judith Auth and Anne Stackpole-Cuellar
Honoring Evacuation from The Sheep Fire, June 2022

Strength

by Joan Koerper (Dr. Mary Joan Koerper)

Grandpa gripped my hand
as we walked
until I flinched and recoiled
telling me to always have a
strong grip and handshake
and never be shy about it.

His lessons helped keep me
strong as I sat between Mom
and Grandpa on the way to
the VA hospital in Ann Arbor
for cancer treatments,
helping hospice him,
and minding the wake,
at the funeral home, for three days
in my shiny patent leather shoes at age six.

I became the best and strongest I could.

Now, older, my hands sometimes fail.
"My hands are no longer strong, Grandpa,"
I whisper to the stars, in the
clear mountain night sky, apologizing.
"It's okay, honey," he replies.
"It happens to us all.
"Strength comes in many forms:
"courage, love, and compassion.
"We are never too frail to carry
those in our hearts and hands."

> In honor of my maternal grandfather
> Walter Albert Burrell
> 9-6-1883 to 10-16-1956

Shadow Reckoning

by Jessica Lea

mind cloud calculating:

want tos

+ have tos

+ need tos

+ forgot tos

+ should haves

= resentments

a Fibonacci sequence of thoughts
spiraling into breathless anxiety

Spirit watches
through winged sisters
circling
casting shadow spells

waiting

look up
breathe
and
come back to now

Birding at Spirit Mountain

BY JESSICA LEA

listen to calls
chirps
cries
songs

train eye to absorb details
memorize plumage
beak shape

hope for a lifer
am I up for the challenge
of competing only with myself

or is it enough to simply say

brother bird
sister spirit
when you soared across the open blue space
between the reaching branches
part of me flew with you
lifted free
and for that moment

no one

was counting

anything

Willingness

BY JESSICA LEA

Do not be afraid
The opposite of fear is love

Rest your burdened weary soul
The opposite of fear is peace

Paths will appear in the wilderness
rivers will flow in the desert

The opposite of fear is faith

Ana's at My Window

by Jessica Lea

Pre-dawn vibration
feathered helicopter lands
on pad of nectar

96 Hours

BY ROBIN WOODRUFF LONGFIELD

On Tuesday, October 9, 2018, after a seizure and fall, my 22-year-old daughter Mia was taken by ambulance from a one-step-from-homelessness trailer park on Higuera Street, San Luis Obispo, California, the nearby French Hospital. She was covered in black, red, and purplish splotches as if someone had beaten the shit out of her. The first responder's assessment of her condition was not promising. Glasgow Coma Scale 3. No response. To anything.

Her " boyfriend" called 911. His neighbors hid Mia's purse and phone from the police. Who thought that was okay? Who, exactly, was this "boyfriend?"

Did anyone even care? Was Mia disposable? Expendable? A sudden liability? What did she know of what had happened to her? What *was* happening to her?

Did she matter to the first responders sent to this south-of-the-skids area of San Luis Obispo? A place where neighbors hid identification and evidence. A place where people saw nothing, heard nothing, and did not answer their doorbells.

Did her condition merit sirens? Was she alone in the back of the ambulance as it ferried her from the one-step-from-home-lessness-trailer park on Higuera Street to French Hospital?

Was there any thought for her at all? By anyone? Or was she already beyond all that?

Mia's disheveled appearance and lack of identification caused the first responders to mistake the All-Star athlete, artist, and would-be crisis counselor for a transient. Was she just another Jane Doe to them? A case number?

Only the work of a social-media-savvy ICU Nurse the following day kept Mia from remaining a Jane Doe. After this sleuthing, the nurse called me at 10:00 a.m. to say that Mia had fallen and sustained a traumatic brain injury. She implored me to gather my family and get to Sierra Vista Medical Center in San Luis Obispo immediately. A Regional Trauma Center. The second hospital to which an ambulance took Mia.

At 7:00 p.m., my husband, Stan, daughter Ariel, and I walked through the ICU doors at Sierra Vista Medical Center. Mia was still unresponsive. A head CT scan reflected no brain activity except in her brainstem. She was gone but for breathing over the ventilator. Life on a ventilator was not what she would have wanted. And so we waited...

Ariel's fiancé, Julian, arrived later that night; Stan's brother Jeff the following morning. Law Enforcement officers were ever-present. A reminder that when it was over, it still was not over.

Two days later, Mia stopped breathing over the ventilator, and a nurse disconnected life support. It was Friday, October 12, 2018.

Our family joined hands while Ariel and I held Mia's hands. We encircled her like a crown—an unbroken circle of broken people. We waited and watched the brightly colored numbers and graphics of the monitors attached to Mia plummet, then stop. Asystole. Over. Done. A detective took Mia away with the respirator apparatus still in place. It was growing dark outside. It was growing darker everywhere.

Red Blanket Sleeper

BY ROBIN WOODRUFF LONGFIELD

After Stan and I signed Hailey's foster-care placement agreement, our social worker, June, left for another appointment. Stan and I rifled through the black trash bag Julia handed to him when we left their house with Hailey earlier in the day.

"I want Hailey to have these things. Before, She arrived at our house with nothing and deserves to leave with at least a little something." Julia had said tearfully to Stan as she handed him the bulging bag.

We turned the bag upside down and emptied it onto the floor. There were two plastic bottles for the baby doll Hailey referred to as "the baby." One contained pretend orange juice, and the other held pretend milk.

Several doll dresses made up the bottom of the pyramid of ephemera at our feet. Matchbox cars and a green-haired troll settled on top of ruffled ankle socks and dresses for church. Pink sneakers, hair styling toys, and a blue ride-on pedal toy that looked like a monster truck comprised the middle of the pile.

At the top of the pyramid was a red blanket sleeper. I removed it from the pile and began to hold it like an heirloom. It was a genuine Dr. Denton, with its patented diagonal zipper. The elastic red and white stripes circling the neckline and wrists reminded me of candy canes. Was this sleeper a Christmas gift? A gift for a December baby? Hailey was a December baby– born on December 26th. What could have been unluckier than that? She was the little gift that Santa quite forgot about and delivered a day late. The baby her birth mother took home and also quite forgot about while chasing the next high and the one after– a trainwreck chasing the train.

Its bright red color was something I would never have chosen for a small child's sleeper. I would not have used it anywhere in a child's bedroom. Any primary color would have been too intense, especially for a child whose beginnings were as rife with trauma as Hailey's.

Its polyester fabric was so pilled and rough that it appeared to have been cleaned by stovetop boiling with lye soap. It didn't smell or feel like fabric softener had ever touched its fibers—no evidence of even the cheapest brand. I imagined detergents like Ariel or Sun passing through its fibers, lifting out stains of every kind imaginable and unimaginable.

I thought more and more about this little sleeper. Who did wear it? Did it once belong to Tommy or Lydia, the now school-age children Duane and Julia adopted as toddlers? It's not likely it came from Hailey's biological mother. I could not imagine anything coming from her unless it was trouble or heartache.

Maybe Julia picked it up at a yard sale, or someone she knew picked it up at a yard sale and gave it to her. People often donated clothing and toys to assist the unending stream of children who came in and out of her home. In their lives as foster parents, nearly 300 children were cared for and loved by Julia and Duane before going on to adoptive parents, a new foster home, or back to their parents or family members. With a license to care only for children from birth to three years old, I imagined she went through kids' clothing the way Hailey's biological mother went through drugs– quickly and cheaply as possible.

I wondered more and more about the history of this little sleeper. How many children loved it, how many did not like it, and how many had no opinion about it? How often was it saturated with the tears of a child who did not particularly want to wear it or go to sleep at that moment? How many dolly, teddy bear, or spaceship secrets did it hear? Did a puppy or kitten snuggle up next to it? What bedtime stories might it have heard? In what languages? Did any of its past experiences penetrate so deeply into the fabric that no amount of washing could remove it?

My musings about the sleeper ended when Hailey awakened from her nap and toddled into the living room. She grabbed the sleeper from me, joyfully proclaiming, "Mine! Mine!"

On that cold, early November night, Hailey and her baby went to sleep together. Hailey in the red blanket sleeper and the baby in a doll-sized sleeper Stan found in the pile of toys and clothing still on the floor.

Hailey outgrew the sleeper; it would last only through one winter. I saved it in an old cedar chest in our attic because of Hailey's immediate and enduring bond with it. The sleeper would not disappoint or abandon her.

Now, Hailey is forever gone from us. The red blanket sleeper outlived her, Julia, and all four grandparents. It also survived the recent summer of downsizing that saw many of the relics of Hailey's life find new lives with family members, children's hospitals, and thrift stores.

The sleeper is preserved in a clear shoe-storage box in the safety of our attic. A bar-soap-sized cedar block keeps it safe from insect intruders. I think of this sleeper in the way one might view a Saint's relic. A second-class relic that touched her, proving she was here and loved. Her miracle was not only in the lives she touched but also in that she survived her early years.

Stan and I are now the curators and keepers of her memory. By preserving what is left to show she lived, by keeping it all safe, we do what no one could do when she lived among us. We keep her essence safe and keep her alive, until we, too, must fade into the memory of those we leave behind.

A Winter's Tale

BY ROBIN WOODRUFF LONGFIELD

My business was mankind, blind, was I—
mankind was my business, was and is.
Blind was I. Beware! Beware! Beware

the starving girl, beware more the boy.
Erase all ignorance from his face.
Leave no trace, erase, erase, erase!

Smoldering skies will suffocate all—
call it what you will, swallow bitter
pills, vomit into community swill.

Rise up and rise again. Mankind, your
business is mankind. Beware the boy!
Beware the angry boy from Leningrad.

Beware, beware, of leaders bearing
Grudges. Their business is Mankind's
Business too. Beware their soulless stares.

Beware their indiscriminate machines
Of death. Beware the lies each missile bears.
Beware more, the lessons left behind—

Beware the hideous inheritance
left to your sons and daughters, inherent
in their eyes—empty, soulless stares.

While poisoned rain drowns Ukraine
while fire falls from the sky, rise up! Rise,
Rise up again! My business was

Mankind, blind was I. Blind too, the power
Besotted boy. He is both yours and mine—
His empire of death belongs to us all.

Beware your hideous inheritance—
Beware the lies each Russian missile bears
As it screams through cities and country towns

Beware! Beware! Beware!

Twilight Bouquets

by Mae Wagner Marinello

The not-quite-full moon hangs in the not-quite-night sky. It is my favorite time of the day, dusk—that time when day is fading into night. The air is cool but not cold and I am picking flowers.

The sweet peas continue to bloom even though some vines are becoming yellow and shriveled and pods are forming their legacy of seeds. Just when I think there will be no more, they burst forth with another colorful splash, another gift for me to savor and share.

The roses, too, are blooming and there is something magical about wending my way through the bushes of thorns and beautiful flowers in the dusky twilight. Bachelor buttons, baby's breath, marigolds and phlox have blossomed from the seeds I scattered in the spring. There is an excitement, a pleasure, as each different flower blooms, each one like a magical mysterious gift unfolding before my eyes. I cannot recognize all of them.

I pick the sweet peas, the roses, the bachelor buttons and baby's breath plus the ones I do not know. I add the pungent marigold and spikes of purple butterfly bush. I carefully snip some bouganveilia with its thorns and bright fuchsia flowers and deep green leaves.

I place each floral harvest on top of the washing machine in the laundry room until I can separate them into bouquets. I prepare and recycle bottles so that I may share the wealth with others. Some are tiny bottles saved for me by my insulin-dependent friend. The fluid that sustains and maintains his health is now the receptacle for another kind of sustenance and replenishment as I prepare these tiny bottles to receive the sweet peas. I remove the labels and pop off the metal tops and they turn into a delicate little vase. For the larger flowers, I recycle other bottles which I often decorate with stickers.

As I work at the washing machine surface, I am reflected in the windows of the laundry room; all daylight has long since disappeared and I feel a sweet pleasure as I separate and mingle flowers into bouquets. I smile, just thinking of how I will give these unexpected bouquets to friends and acquaintances and even to an occasional stranger. They will smile and lift the bottle to their face to drink in the fragrance of the sweet pea.

And this, this time of day, along with the flowers—especially the sweet peas—is how and when I would want to be remembered by all who might have known and loved me.

Help

by Mae Wagner Marinello

It was 1970 and I was sitting in a storefront welfare office next to a Stater Brothers market on Mission Boulevard in Rubidoux. I was waiting to apply for help. At the reception desk sat an older, bosomy lady wearing a lavender dress that complemented her silver-gray hair. "Jesus Loves You" promised a sign sitting on her desk. Maybe Jesus loved us but she did not look like she did. She sat there, looking aloof, cold, distant.

The waiting room was filled with people. My baby daughter was on my lap—I wouldn't let her down on the germy floor to play with who-knows-where-they'd-been germy toys. A gaunt, elderly gentleman sat nearby. The worn belt around his thin waist was way too large for him and was flipped back through several of the loops. At one point, he got up, left the building, and soon returned with a pound cake from Stater's. He ripped the package open and hungrily began cramming cake into his mouth, yellow crumbs cascading down his shirt and scattering onto the floor. When the name "Mr. Hamilton" was called, he rose and disappeared into the maze of cubicles beyond the reception desk. I felt great sadness, wondering if "Mr. Hamilton" had once been dignified, respected, and not hungry to the point of desperation.

Another young mother with two small children and I conversed at length until they called my name. The person who interviewed me was a stern-looking older man. His eyes were icy and cold as he peered over his glasses, looking me up and down. Was I pregnant *again*, he wanted to know. After all, I had a baby on my lap, I was applying for food stamps and obviously didn't have a lick of sense about anything. I felt stripped naked, vulnerable, ashamed, worthless and stupid.

I was there because my then-pastor emphatically told me I needed help. And my six-year-old son had asked "is this all we have to eat again?"

I knew then I had to swallow my pride and ask for help.

The icy-eyed man could not have known how happily I thought I was married, that the baby on my lap had been conceived in love just like her two brothers, ages five and six. That I never dreamed my husband of 11 years would have an affair during my pregnancy, leaving me devastated and suicidal with new baby blues, three children and no money. After all, I thought I was going to live happily ever after. How could I, *me*, be sitting here in a welfare office?

But I was.

Finally, the ordeal over, I returned to the sanctuary of my home, located on Riverview Drive, a major thoroughfare through Rubidoux. Later in the afternoon, I saw the woman I had spoken to walking along the embankment above my front yard. She must have already walked at least two miles, coming from the welfare office. She was carrying one child and trying to hang onto the hand of the other. I called out to her and asked what had happened to the ride who was supposed to pick her up. She said she didn't know and could I call him? She didn't want to leave the side of the road in case he passed by on his way to get her.

In answer to a stranger's phone call, he told me his truck had broken down.

I offered to take her home. After all, I still had a car. It must have been a good 15 miles to where she was staying and a light rain had begun to fall. As we rode along, she said, "I don't know what I would have done without you. God brought you to me today."

Fifty-two years later, I don't know if she remembers me—but the memory of her is indelibly branded into my psyche. I meant to help her. Instead, she is the one who helped me when she spoke those words—"God brought you to me today."

Help, in whatever form it takes, has the power to alter lives forever.

One Wild Ride

by Terry Lee Marzell

On our Carnival cruise to Mexico in December, 2022, Hal and I signed up for a shore excursion to ride ATVs—all-terrain vehicles—in Cabo San Lucas. We'd never done that before, and the daytrip sounded like it might be fun. But let me tell you, that experience was one wild ride—and I was the one driving!

As my wardrobe for this excursion, I chose a pair of elastic-waist jeans with plenty of give, a button-down blouse, and tennis shoes. Around my waist, I tied a zipper-front hoodie with *Columbus Ohio* emblazoned across the front. When I mounted my four-wheeled motorcycle, slinging my travel purse crossbody in front of me and donning my mandatory safety helmet, I felt for all the world like the world's coolest senior citizen biker chick.

It didn't take long to master the mechanics involved in driving the ATV. No fancy gears—just a simple go, stop, turn left, and turn right. No problema. The eleven of us turistas were directed to form a line and drive in single file throughout the excursion. There was no danger of getting lost, with trail boss Luis in the lead and wrangler Rogelio bringing up the rear.

However, my confidence only lived for about fifty feet. It evaporated when Luis decided to kick it into high gear and, with a roar of his engine, hurtle down the unpaved path at breakneck speed, leaving the rest of us in a cloud of dust. I was positioned towards the end of the line, but even so far from the front, I nearly choked on his dirt tornado.

Before long, though, I was zipping along the sandy path at a dizzyingly high speed, jockeying over chuckholes, careening around hairpin turns, lurching over rocks bigger than a breadbox, dodging prickly bramble that lined both sides of the trail, and otherwise jeopardizing my own life and limb. In my effort to keep up with the group, I had to drive recklessly fast, and I struggled to stay astride the vehicle. How long would it be, I wondered, before this mechanical beast would finally rebel and pitch me unceremoniously into the thorny thicket?

Before long, the serpentine path opened up into a wide, sandy field, allowing me a clear view of two riders ahead of me—a teenage girl and a young man. I cast a quick glance backward and spotted a forty-something woman behind me and Rogelio behind her. But where were the others, who at the start of the ride had been visible ahead of us?

Suddenly, the teenaged girl veered off to the right, the rest of us following close on her tail. She speedily approached a small berm, plowed over some downed barbed wire and a sign that lay face down and was therefore unreadable, lurched over the berm, and traversed a small rivulet. Then she sped away, off-off-road, across the Sonoran chaparral.

Before those of us behind her could do the same, Rogelio zoomed around us, dashed up to the berm, and came to a screeching halt. "Ay, Dios mío!" he muttered. He bellowed after the girl, "Hey! Lady! Come back! Hey!" But she couldn't hear him over the roar of multiple engines.

Rogelio jumped off his ATV and hollered to the three of us, "You three wait here!" Then he jumped over the barbed wire, scrambled over the berm, jumped the rivulet, and sprinted way on foot across the Mexican desert to corral the wayward teenager.

As the three of us waited, our machines now puttering on idle, I took the opportunity to make some necessary wardrobe repairs—I pulled up my pants, pulled down my blouse, tightened my hoodie, and re-adjusted my crossbody purse. Less and less was I feeling like that cool biker chick. I scanned the terrain up and down and all around. Where was Luis? Where was the group? Where was my husband? Obviously, those of us at the end of the line had become separated from the rest of the herd.

"Well," I chuckled, "Looks like Luis has lost control of the class."

The forty-something woman behind me let out a small groan. "She's my daughter," the lady moaned. "The girl Rogelio went running after—she's my daughter."

"Oh, my," I returned. "Well, as a retired schoolteacher, I can tell you, there's always one maverick in every class." This observation was small comfort to the apprehensive mother. Oh, yes, you can always count on me to say just the right thing when there is a situation.

"Don't worry," I said soothingly, attempting to mend my oopsie. "Rogelio will find her and bring her back." The three of us sat in silence, our machines softly rumbling, for what seemed like an interminable length of time, but which could have only been five or six minutes.

Suddenly, the missing ATV burst from the brushwood, carrying both Rogelio and the girl. When they reached the rivulet, Rogelio jumped off, leaped over the watery ditch, stumbled over the berm and the barbed wire, and climbed aboard his own mount.

"Follow me!" he shouted, and then the wrangler took off—muy, muy rápido.

At length we discovered the rest of the group waiting for us on the Mexican shoreline, casually enjoying the view. My husband ran up to me and confessed that he'd had an accident—he rear-ended the ATV in front of him, which happened to be driven by the forty-something woman's *other* daughter. Nice. As I mentally composed an apology for the woman and some sort of explanation for the insurance agent, Hal chuckled. "Don't worry—there wasn't any damage." Ah, qué bueno.

After a few minutes, trail boss Luis rounded everyone up and readied to move us all out. He approached me and directed me to fall in behind him, and he told Hal to position himself behind me. Why? I wondered. Why was it *me* being moved to the front of the group, like a disobedient school-child in need of extra supervision? I wasn't the one who went riding off into the western frontier! And I wasn't the bumper-car driver, either.

"Did I do something wrong?" I asked. But, unfortunately, Luis's command of the English language was limited. My command of Spanish was even less so. "Estoy mala?" I finally managed to stammer. "No, not at all," he assured me. Well, OK, I thought, still confused as Luis jumped on his ATV and bolted away like a thoroughbred racehorse right out of the gate. Obviously, this is not a man who learns from the mistakes of his students.

Following in hot pursuit, I impelled roughshod up a steep bluff containing more chuckholes, more hairpin turns, and more rocks bigger than a breadbox. Spiny bushes snagged and scraped my arms as I sped by, and several times I had to swerve to avoid getting scratched in the face. My ATV had become a bucking bronco, and, amigos, this was indeed my first rodeo. Nevertheless, I managed to stay in the saddle and keep up. "You were smokin' your husband!" Rogelio said to me later. Again, I was just trying to keep up.

Once we reached the summit of the bluff, Luis puttered to a stop, parked, and dismounted. We turistas did the same. Gazing westward, we were richly rewarded with a dazzling view of the Pacific Ocean that stretched before us all the way to the horizon. Frothy waves gently washed the shore-line at the bottom of the bluff below. Salt spray perfumed the air. And then, we spotted a pod of migrating whales gliding noiselessly down the coast. Qué magnífico!

When we finally rolled into camp later that afternoon, I was jubilant. I had entered the ring and emerged a rodeo champion. Hal and I dismounted our equus mechanicus, slipped off our safety helmets, and wobbled to the watering hole—not to get a drink, but to wash the grit off our hands and faces.

"That was one wild ride," I declared to my husband, who nodded in agreement. Then we gave each other a wide grin. "Let's do that again!" we exclaimed in unison.

The Pen

BY TERRY LEE MARZELL

The pen is placed on the page,
And the ink flows from the tip.
Words belligerent and sage,
Which would never pass the lip.

Valentine's Day 2017

BY PHYLLIS MAYNARD

The sunshiny start of Valentine's Day in 2017 hinted of possible surprises ahead! But, by 11 A.M. that day, the surprise was on me!

The line dance class at Goeske Senior Center was just winding down with learning a new dance (Neon Nights). Now, as I was negotiating a turn, what was formerly right foot-left foot became two left feet and down I plummeted, thinking on the way down, "If I can just land on my backside, it'll not hurt or harm, since that's where the ample padding has always been located." I fell very "easily" "quietly"...just sort of "rolled" and ended up letting my backside take the fall, gently bumping my head on the floor.

This concerned me—I've always valued my head more than my back side and didn't welcome any above-the-neck damage. I felt OK and tried to scramble to my feet, lessening the embarrassment I was feeling. But, wait!!..where the heck is my right leg??? It isn't there! At least the feeling isn't there! My friends gathered around me—helping me to a chair and then began their diagnosing—the leg? The ankle? The back?? One friend swore she could see the right leg shorter than the left!! And, of course it was impossible to place any pressure on my right leg. The ambulance arrived shortly after some wise guy called 911, and OH—the mortification of being hauled on a gurney through Goeske Center like a load of potatoes!

Now, from time to time we have all witnessed the 911 departures from the senior center and all the tongue cluckings and teeth suckings seemed appropriate accompaniment to my dramatic exit.

The ride to Kaiser Hospital was almost pleasant, since there was no pain whatsoever (I was sure this was all a big mistake and my problem would only be a pinched nerve!) At the hospital the questions began:

When did this happen? Where did this happen? How did this happen?

What? Line dancing? Did you say line dancing? Were you dizzy? Line dancing, you say?

Has this happened before? Line dancing,hummmmmmmmm

I was no longer feeling like an energetic, active, senior citizen but now felt like a statistic---taking "THE FALL" while pursuing a healthy, fun, pastime.

At the hospital I was hustled into the emergency area where the doctors did a quick scan of my situation and decided the damage was done to my right leg and HIP! (My leg AND HIP!! Oh no, that sounds like more than a pinched nerve!!!)

Anxiety was moving in when I began thinking that even with all the king's horses and all the king's men, me and Humpty Dumpty were headed for the same finale.

Later that day my ill-fated Valentine surprise began looking less dismal and all the worry and fretting seemed unnecessary as the good doctors at Kaiser Hospital performed their wizardly feats to put me together again!!!!!!!

Shopping Cheap

BY PHYLLIS MAYNARD

Merry Christmas to all and
to all a good-night. I've
turned off my brain and my
eyes are shut tight

I've run out of vigor
I'm all out of vim
I've checked all my gift lists
for her and for him

Each one has been gifted
with trinkets or cash
I've tried to be frugal.
Tried not to be rash

Each name on my list
holds a spot in my heart,
and our mutual esteem runs deep
and I've tried (REALLY TRIED)
–but it's hard at the start,
to shop without buying cheap!

Merry Greenbacks

by Phyllis Maynard

I'd give you the stars,
and the moon I'd ensnare
but if I could
and if I dare,
...your stockings that hang by the chimney with care
would bulge at the seams with greenbacks to spare!

Two Little Old Ladies

BY PHYLLIS MAYNARD

Two little old ladies—well into their eighties,
would meet every Monday for lunch.
They thought it was fun — to go on the run,
and find a cheap place to munch.
They opted for venues that boasted their menus
were clean, tasty, and cheap.
McDonald's offer of "only a buck" they
found was a bid hard to beat! McChicken!
they sang — as the register rang "One dollar
and nine cents to pay"
for this tasty treat (a snack hard to beat!)
in the middle part of the day!
Then, on to "The Tree" (Dollar Tree, you see)
was ecstasy beyond measure.
To shop for doo-dads and trinkets and "things"
that two old gals could treasure!

Taking a Gamble

by Mary McLoughlin

Thought to take a gamble
Down an unknown road for a wee ramble
The road curved round and round
until it went through a patch of bramble

Those stickers did really smart
Scratched my legs and tore my socks
But that was ok got away
Scarred forever what can I say

On and on did traverse
Determined not to give in or my course to reverse
Around the next bend met an old man who was rude and terse
Kept moving and in my head uttered a silent curse!
So all to be done was take out this notebook and jot down a verse!

In conclusion and to divest of any confusion
The gamble of the ramble
was fun not a shamble!

Growing Old

BY MARY MCLOUGHLIN

Been told
At this age I'm growing old

Funny, don't feel old
Maybe dementia is settling in
Still think I'm young and thin

Decided to ignore the truth
Play my drum, learn the uke
Chat with friends, hike the hills

Play with my grandkids
(while they still want to play with me!)
Watch the clouds, be amazed by the sea
Read a book in the shade of a tree

Isn't it great to be alive!

The Shell

by Mary McLoughlin

A grandson is fantastic, magical
and great
Such a wonderful beau for an afternoon date

Around Lake Gregory we walked and talked
Prodded and investigated
So much to see and examine
Objects and animals there was no famine
He is nine!

So fine
full of life and new life to me infuses

A shell he found and carried it around
On the way home he asks
'Do like it, granny?'
'Yes'
'Granny, this treasure is yours'
'I know' I said

Helen

BY MARY McLOUGHLIN

My dear Helen where have you gone
You've been away for so very long
A part of me has gone too....

My dear Helen, you were my song!

We spent our youth together
Remember the flat?
Two years of madness, fun and all that

Born an ocean apart
But in minds and hearts we were twined
As if we were twins at the start!

We made our gallant, girlish plans
They're now gone like the winds of sand

Met my Frank
For that, you I thank

A vivid dream of you woke me one day
Oh, so sure you were coming back to stay
You did, but not I thought was the way
The news came that afternoon my dearest darling

Helen, you had passed away!

But Helen you're only 23
Far too young and alive not to survive

Helen, love to you I send
And hope for a heaven to see you again, my dear friend!

Clothes Pins

by Mary McLoughlin

Some call them pins, some prefer pegs
Some have springs, some have legs
Some end up clips for bags of chips
Or holding open pages for in a book
for a musician or a cook!

But their favorite place is on a line
Where they work so very fine
Most of the time!

The washing machine was a scrubbing board in a metal sink
Soap and rub the sheets up and down lost in thoughts, time to
    think!
Soap the pillow slips, towels and smalls in that cold water sink!

Scrub hard, knuckles red and skinned
Rinse in the zinc sink looking at fields, stone walls, cows
    grazing, sheds and byres
Squeeze with all my might!

Wellie boots on on the way to the back field and the clothes line
Plenty of pegs and wet clothes in a metal tub
Remove the wood pole hiking the line up to catch the wind
Making it easy to hang the wash and peg it to the line
Stretch the sheets and use plenty of pegs

White and pink sheets and pillow slips hung gingerly with more
    pegs
These sheets were wedding gifts!

Hawk the line up to the sky with the pole
Catching the wind do its thing

But this is the wild Atlantic coast
The end of winter morphing into spring
Later, the breeze turned blustery, then gale force!
Rain came down in buckets, lashing
Huge drops beat the ground, window washing!
Oh no! In the back field the sheets wound around!

Never did find those sheets even after tramping all the fields
    around
All the way down to the briny sea
Those pegs let me down
The sheets sailed far out on the sea somewhere else to be!

And those pegs still on the line, just seemed to smile at me!

The Sweet and Savory Tamal

by Rose Y. Monge

I look forward to Alaina Bixon's food workshop every semester. It allows me to expand my writing in addition to facilitating the memoir class at the Goeske Center. Alaina introduces the term "food anthropology" at the beginning of the semester and the term intrigues me. She explains that there's a major interest now with the origins or anthropology of food. She adds that "we define ourselves by the food we eat when we were youngsters."

What is "food anthropology?" The website: https://www.hackensackmeridianhealth.org/en/ defines it as "more than an analysis of food in culture." It goes beyond food as nutrition. "It has a cultural dimension by which people choose what they eat not only by flavor or nutritional value but cultural, religious, historic, economic or social status, and environmental factors.

Alaina encourages us to research the origins of the food we eat. Since the holidays are rapidly approaching, my mind wanders to food celebrations during the holidays. For my family, the Christmas Eve feast must include tamales.

Why tamales? Found in Mexico and in Central and South America, tamales are a traditional Latin American dish made of cornmeal dough (called masa) filled with meats, cheeses, or dried fruit. In fact, you can make tamales with any filling. Tamales are wrapped in corn husks, banana leaves, or other wrappings before steaming.

I wrote the following story decades ago before Mom's passing. As I review it, it brings so many memories of Mom, my siblings and my younger self.

The "Tamalada"

BY ROSE Y. MONGE

The tamale quest begins after Halloween. Mom and I look for sales and bargains and buy in bulk. Items are stored in her big freezer and pantry. Corn husks are not a staple year-round therefore we buy them when available for they are in high demand particularly after Thanksgiving. Nowadays with the emerging diverse population in the Inland Empire, many stores are addressing the need to diversify their grocery offerings.

The ingredients for tamales are unlimited. Every family has a cherished recipe passed down by family members. Tamales are both savory and sweet. The Monge tamales consists of masa, corn husks and meat items cooked with red chili sauce. Any meat product is acceptable such as pork, beef and chicken. Sweet tamales run the gamut of fruit variations. It might appear that with so few ingredients the recipe is simple, but the challenge comes in its execution, for every procedure must be done just right to ensure success.

I must admit that I haven't mastered all the steps in the art of tamale making. With so many years under mom's tutelage, I should be a tamale guru but I'm not. We prepare fifteen to twenty dozen at a time which are eaten throughout the holidays. Mom always keeps extra for unexpected guests.

The date is set for us to meet prior to Christmas at Mom's for the "tamalada." Sisters Mary and Norma plus sister-in-law, Kathy, and I arrive in the morning and plan to stay the entire day and into the evening devoted to the endeavor. Mom's small kitchen can be chaotic with so many of us working simultaneously but we manage. We laugh and tell jokes and just enjoy each other's company. Mom's loving and gentle guidance is omnipresent, but we all have a hand in the final product.

We begin by roasting the meat in the oven. Expensive cuts of meat are not needed since the slow process will tenderize even the most inexpensive cuts. The roast cooks for hours with water or broth, a little salt and plenty of garlic. Once the desired tenderness is achieved, we shred, cover and set it aside. Chicken is prepared in the same manner. The broth of both items is reserved to add to the chili sauce and the masa. Packages of dried and ground New Mexico and California Red Chiles, garlic, a little salt, white flour, and cooking oil are the ingredients for the sauce. Fresh garlic cloves are sautéed in the oil followed by the flour and chili powders. Adding the broth at intervals brings it to its desired consistency. The last step is to combine the shredded meat with the chili sauce. Mom's culinary signature is to add black olives and raisins.

While the meat is cooking, we make the masa. Fresh masa is available now at many markets, but mom makes her own using the brand Maseca. With her guidance, I combine the flour, salt, some baking powder, lard and then the chicken broth in increments creating a good texture for spreading. I blend all ingredients by hand.

Others clean and soak the husks and separate them. Soaking them for hours makes them easier to fold and are kept in water until they are ready for use. The soaked husks have a smooth and a rough side. The latter is always on the outside of the tamale. The smooth side is patted dry before we spread the masa. We use a spatula or a large spoon in a downward motion on the wider side of the husk; the narrower side will be folded over. It's important to spread evenly and not too thick for it will cook unevenly. This is not my forte and I take the teasing from the savvy spreaders in stride.

The meat mixture is placed carefully in the middle of the husk about one fourth from the top. A second or third husk is wrapped over the meat, folding the narrow tip to close it. It's important that no meat or masa escapes from any of the folded sides. Once assembled, we place them in storage bags by the dozen in the freezer. We rejoice in exhaustion once we cross the finish line.

On Christmas Eve, everyone gathers at Mom's throughout the day. Mom defrosts dozens of tamales the previous day. Savory and spicy odors permeate the tiny kitchen. Steam arises from the deep cooking pots or ollas used for cooking beans. Our Nana (grandmother) used water-soaked kitchen towels to cover the tamales, but Mom uses aluminum foil. A large, deep ceramic bowl is placed upside down to form a small dome in the center. A small amount of water is added to cover the bottom of the bowl. Too much water may touch the tamales making them soggy or cause them to unravel.

Tamales are stacked snuggly side by side around the plate in a an upward circular pattern. More foil is loosely positioned on top before closing the lid. The slow cook in medium heat takes two hours or more. Water is added regularly to keep that level of heat. The magic is in the steam. After a few hours, Mom takes one of the tamales from the top of the pot and lets it sit for a minute or two. If the masa is firm to the touch, they are ready to eat.

The small kitchen takes center stage. Two pots of tamales are steaming on the stove-ready to be eaten: a large pot for the meat and a smaller one for the chicken. There is no formal seating, and we eat at our own leisure. Family potluck dishes complete the meal. After years of potlucks, each of us bring our "signature" offerings. I am the appetizer and dessert girl. My brother, Rudy owns the chiles rellenos and the guacamole. Little sis, Norma delights us with a green salad; older sister, Mary is the queen of Spanish rice. Sister-in-law Kathy has perfected potato salad. The meal is not complete without Mom's home-made frijoles and fresh salsa.

We eat and socialize throughout the evening. Opening gifts will follow at midnight in the living room cluttered with presents around the Christmas tree. Sister Sally from San Francisco and brother Harvey from Santa Barbara and their families will visit us later during the holiday season.

Mom typically rewards me with two dozen tamales which I share with my friends after the holidays. I am thankful that Mom keeps this family tradition alive and hope that one day I will be as proficient as she in the art of tamale making.

Post-Script.

Sadly, after Mom's passing in 2011, the tamalada becomes a treasured memory but no longer a focus for the holiday preparations. We still celebrate on Christmas Eve but now meet at my brother Rudy's home. I appreciate that my sister-in-law, Kathy, keeps the tamale tradition alive honoring Mom's recipe. She makes the tamales at home and brings them for everyone to enjoy on Christmas Eve. I miss the camaraderie with my family as only three of my siblings keep regularly in touch. I understand. They are busy with their grandkids, have medical issues or live out of the area. The nieces and nephews are adults with children of their own and are setting up their own traditions. Will we ever have another tamalada? Who knows?

Did I master the art of tamales? Nope.

A Race Around the Kitchen

by Barbara Mortensen

Nothing excites me more than the sound of a great race car! Yes, I am addicted to Formula One Grand Prix car racing. The sound of these great engineered cars is sometimes as rapturous to me as the sound of a great symphony.

To my great delight, I was living in São Paulo when one of the early Formula One races in Brasil was going to be held at Interlagos, one of the nicest lakeside areas in São Paulo.

I was excited to be so close to the event and happy to know that the teams were going to be staying at the São Paulo Hilton, the hotel I had called home until I permanently settled into my gorgeous apartment.

I was lucky to have maintained all of my friendships with the incredible staff at the hotel. They were my mainstay for so long, while I adjusted to living in a country I never had known, speaking a language I had to learn. Imagine: me, an adult, having to ask someone how to write out a check so that I could pay a bill!

So back to Formula One: On race day, Sunday, my newly installed phone began to ring. When I answered, it was the fabulous Regine from the hotel, who knew everyone and did everything for them and was one of the best-loved characters in all of São Paulo!

Why was she calling? Well, the dry cleaners and the laundry at the hotel were closed on Sunday, and they couldn't locate anyone to run the laundry or the dry cleaners at the last minute.

Why was this so important? Well, the race car drivers wear wool garments, something like long johns, that protect them from fire and keep their bodies insulated. These intimate wool garments had to be washed and cleaned before the race.

Regine knew that I had a washing machine and a dryer. She

asked whether I would be able to wash and dry these garments in time for the race. Of course, I said we (my household help and I) would try.

Regine, my cook and I turned my fabulous kitchen into a laundry and proceeded to wash and dry these precious life-saving garments.

However, my dryer could not accommodate all of the items at one time, and we really had a deadline! We opened my oven door and loaded as many of the items as could fit and "baked" them dry.

We laughed and thought about our "cooking" for the day. We met the deadline. The drivers had their "clean cooked garments" and my kitchen was once again the home of great food aromas.

Shared Meals

BY BARBARA MORTENSEN

I was staying at my brother's house after my recent arrival from my beloved Brasil. One afternoon I was "cooking." Actually, I was making soup. I cut up all the vegetables he had on hand, carrots, celery, onions (the famous trio), mixed vegetables, beans, potatoes, rice, pasta, basically everything he had in his house, including leftover meat and bones. I added vegetable broth and water and lit the stove.

Soon, the kitchen had this wonderful aroma. As the soup cooked, my brother's friends arrived. They couldn't get over the wonderful warm, comforting smells and asked where they were coming from. I told them that I was cooking soup. They asked if they could have a taste of the soup once it was done.

Well, not only did they taste it, they liked it so much, they ate the entire 8-quart pot of soup!

So, I had to start all over again making soup, or else I would not have food for my precious dogs to eat! You see, the soup I was making was for my dogs!

Why?

Well, when I lived in Brasil, my veterinarian advised me that if I wanted my dogs to thrive, I should "cook soup" for them, as the commercial dog food in Brasil was not up to his high standards.

What seems like a million years and many dogs later, I still make "dog soup," and I always make enough so that my family and my guests and my dogs can all share a meal together.

Peter and the Priest

by Barbara Mortensen

He was round and bald with cherry red cheeks. He looked like the stereotypical cherub except that he was over 6 feet tall.

He was the favorite Catholic priest in Key West Florida. Why? He was the only local priest embracing the gay community who, at the time, were largely fighting the onset of AIDS or had AIDS and were living their last moments of life in a warm climate.

He was shunned by other priests and other Catholic families who didn't understand the plague that affected so many young people, mainly gay men who were living in the midst of their community.

He didn't care about the reprimands from his diocese or from other worshippers. He was a true believer and a most righteous person who believed in true mercy!

My best friend Peter was raised in a very Catholic but warm and welcoming household. All of his life until the Catholic church took a negative position towards "Gays" and especially sick gays, he was a proper practicing Catholic who loved his religion and savored all the traditions and practices common to his beloved church. When he found that he was no longer welcome, Peter joined the Metropolitan Community church who did welcome Gay men whether or not they were well or infirmed.

But remember, I was telling you the story about how I met this wonderful priest.

Peter was on his "death bed." I had made a promise to Peter many years before: if anything ever happened to him, I would take care of him and take care of whatever needs he or his loving family had.

It was the time for me to keep my promise. We, Peter, and his fabulous supportive family were in Key West spending the last of

Peter's life being together. His family went to mass every day. The church they attended was the church in which my cherubic priest served.

One morning, as Peter lay dying in his bed, his parents and brothers and sisters in law and I were having breakfast. His parents asked me if, knowing how Peter felt about the Catholic church, whether I thought it would be all right to have last rites said for Peter. They were asking me, the Jewish lady raised in a semi-orthodox Jewish household if it was ok to have this very traditional Catholic service for Peter. Of course, my answer was a resounding YES! Soon after breakfast Peter's family went to church to make the proper arrangements.

His family returned from church and said that the priest would arrive later that afternoon to say last rites for our beloved Peter. I could see the comfort on their faces knowing that traditions they lived by were going to be embraced for their loving son.

The priest arrived and when he greeted me he said that "he knew all about me and what I had done and what I was doing, and he knew that I was Jewish but would I be offended if he said a prayer for me?" "Of course, he could": was my answer: as long as the prayer for me wasn't last rites! I was truly honored and proud to accept this very lovely token of esteem.

We, the priest, Peter's brothers, sisters in law and parents went to Peter's room. Peter's father and the priest were standing on one side of the bed. The rest of his family were either at the foot of the bed or next to me on the other side of the bed.

All of a sudden Peter's father and the priest broke out in laughter! I thought to myself "hmm, this isn't usually the way last rites start but what did I know?" They began pointing at me and the entire family began to laugh. Why?

Let me confess: Inadvertently I was wearing a hot pink tee shirt Peter bought for me some time ago that said, and I quote: "PUT SOMETHING EXCITING BETWEEN YOUR LEGS". Not a typical tee shirt nor one you would expect someone to be wearing during this sacred ritual.

To explain, the tee shirt came from a bicycle shop in Key West and I forgot that I was wearing it. It broke all the tension in the room and brought us all closer together. Later that day, my cherubic priest who stayed with us for the rest of the evening approached me, his 4th or 5th double scotch in hand, and thanked me for giving Peter's family this very special gift. "Au contraire" I said holding my own scotch in hand, "you are the one to be thanked."

To this day, some 40 years later, I still have that very special tee shirt. Once in a while when I feel nostalgic, I pull it out and wear it on my bicycle ride.

Second Hope

by Jane O'Shields

Hope is the bird's nest
my son brought, one autumn day.
Smoke clouds covering.
Hills burning. Flaming fingers
lapping at the trunks of trees.

He ran toward me that
afternoon when fear drifted
through the air. I stood under
a live oak tree, poised.
Students holding pencils.

I watched him sprint from
the top of the hill, slowing
to a walk before pausing,
carefully placing the nest
in my hands, then smiling and
running away.

The night we unpacked, the
bird's nest was gone.

Yesterday, in the
gloom of a cool April day
my son threw open the door.
He walked toward me where
I sat, writing, beside a
hearth fire, flaming.

Holding a cradle
of twigs and down in his small,
strong hands, knowing I would thrill
at the sight. I would laugh out
loud. I would open my hands.

Wooly down warmed my
palms, my chilled, lonesome
fingers, like fire never could.
My son filled my heart with his
sprint and his smile. My son filled
my hands with his hope.

for Joseph

This was published in *Offerings*, Tiferet's Poetry Anthology
with poems by participants in Tiferet writing workshops from
2020-2022.

My Senior Addiction

BY BONNIE PARMENTER

Retiring after a lengthy teaching career, I was slammed with a cluster of life crises including the death of both my parents and my second divorce after 20 years of marriage. The structure of life collapsed for me. Just staying in bed all day was a temptation, but it seemed like I might never get up again. The zombie-walk of grief left me searching for some activity that might bring some color back into my life again. One day I watched a young boy seeming to make cartoon creatures do his bidding with his TV control. I was in fifth grade before I even saw a television set, so this was magical, and I was hooked.

I became a video game addict. However, my games are and are not what you visualize. My gateway game was Naughty Dog's *Crash Bandicoot and the Wrath of Cortex*. I loved saying the name of the game. It was so popular that when a new bandicoot fossil was discovered, they named it *Crash*.

Despite my post retirement malaise, in the video world, I was bright orange and adventurous, meeting quirky characters and wandering imaginary lands with appealing alliterative names. I slid across ice, bounced off elephants' heads, water skied and dodged poison penguins. At first, I was awkward with the controls, but unlike the regular world, there was total privacy and no competition and I kept getting better.

Having my character die still made me feel sad and guilty. In the ice world, when Crash slipped into the water and turned into an ice cube with a pathetic moan, I wanted to apologize. In many games, the only way to conquer a challenge is to go as fast as possible, and I had to work to overcome my cautious nature. I am also stubborn. I was convinced that I could eventually learn how to jump, race and dodge. *I can do this! I can do this!* Many times I was shocked to discover that it was 2 am. Each day I could see progress in my eye-to-hand coordination, something I was not known for. I would work for hours unsuccessfully, only to sleep on it and the next day discover that I could do it. Day after day, I could see the evidence of the "neuroplasticity" of my old brain.

When I say video games, most people picture ugly, violent games. *Grand Theft Auto* has a bad reputation but I just had to try it. It is ugly but genuinely well built. The problem is that your avatar is very weak at the beginning and only gains skill and strength as the game progresses. In GTA, a weak character on the streets of LA gets called the ugliest set of words that you have ever heard, ones that I had sent kids to the office for year after year. I had to suppress the urge to fill out a referral to the principal on myself for even hearing them. My solution was to turn the sound off and work my way through the challenges of the first hours. Once I had enough street cred, the name calling subsided and I could zip around the streets, stealing cars, solving puzzles, and discovering new territories without being verbally eviscerated. The map echoes LA and San Francisco. I was fascinated at how it could feel so familiar. When my next task was to steal a huge plane and fly it over the city, I quit. That sounded too dangerous.

The years passed, color came back to day to day living and my addiction subsided.

Then, knowing that I am The Crazy Cat Lady, my third-is-the-charm husband bought me a game called *Stray* with a nimble, amazingly realistic feline as the avatar. It has the traditional varieties of environments and forgiving death reboots. The challenges are puzzles and hidden spaces in dark corners that light up like bits of lost jewelry called "memories" which I have never totally retrieved. Because I love watching the grace and skill of the cat, I keep going back. Trying to get a perfect score is always such a temptation. There's a zone of concentration where time and worry fall away and all that's left is the joy of surfing your brain activity. Game builders know how addictive that is.

I know my fascination approaches the level of addiction, and I am grateful that it is neither illegal nor immoral. Although immoral has a certain amusing appeal. Of course, it turns out to be a long way from prudent. There is always the lure of the latest game and the newest platform to play it on. Over the years I have played a surprisingly long list of games. Looking back over my life gives me the same feeling of surprise. I like to think that working at each new adventure in life has increased my skills, though I am ironically aware that some of the skills may not be useful to me in this lifetime. In video games, the avatar dies endlessly and always rejuvenates, creating a false sense of invincibility. Readers and writers of fiction will recognize the attraction of that concept.

"Rebooting" after each of my divorces has been an infuriating death both times, though it has given me the false impression that a death is followed by an interesting new life. The final death I face here on earth may not be like that. Ah, but then again, maybe it will!

Shuffling Off to Buffalo

BY CHRISTINE PETZAR

Saturday morning at the dance studio while my granddaughter is in hip-hop class. The tide of parents rushing in to drop off kids is flowing out again, on their phones coordinating the next errand. I remember those years—things to do, places to go. Barbecues, birthday parties, sports practices and games, school plays and performances. Glad that time is over, if I'm honest.

It's quiet now. Just a few of us from "the grandparent brigade" reading or making small talk, occasionally glancing through the window to watch our grandkids in action. We're not in a hurry. My eye lands on the bulletin board of activities.

Hmm… there's an adult tap class on Wednesday nights.

—Oh, come on, who are you kidding? You're 63 years old.

Yeah, but it might be worth checking out.

—You haven't danced since fourth grade. You weren't graceful then and are even less so now. And your sister was always better than you anyway. Admit it.

Yeah, but I have a good sense of timing and rhythm.

—You also have a bad back.

Yeah, but I love those tap dancing movies with Shirley Temple and Fred Astaire and Gene Kelly. I can dream, can't I?

—You think you're "42nd Street" material?? Puh-leeze.

No…but I could try it out at least. Nothing ventured, nothing gained.

—Sure. Go ahead. What have you got to lose? Only your dignity. You'll look ridiculous. Don't say I didn't warn you.

* Ten Years Later *

Saturday morning. Walking over to a neighbor's house to drop something off. Kids doing cartwheels in the front yard. A boy who's about eight calls out:

—Why aren't you walking with one of those stick things?

You mean a cane? Why do you think I need a cane? Is it my white hair?

—No, you have an old face. (No malice, just a statement of fact. Can't argue with it.)

—Can you do this? (He launches into a cartwheel.)

No, but can you do this? I launch into a couple of time-steps, some buffalos, and

throw in a moonwalk.

—Stunned silence. Mind. Blown.

Dignity intact.

Chris and the Karmann Ghia

by Christine Petzar

I learned to drive on my mother's Karmann Ghia. If you've never seen one, it's a Volkswagen that's smaller than a Beetle. It was a tiny car for three growing kids, twisting ourselves into the back seat like contortionists in some clown car. And its baby blue color added to the impression that this was not a serious car. My brother joked about buying mag wheels and driving to the burger joint near the high school where the tough kids hung out. He also floated the idea of crafting a mouse tail from coat hangers and attaching it to the back with a pink bow. It's the only car we ever named—Peggy Sue. The inspiration was a Disney animated short called *Susie the Little Blue Coupe*, but it morphed into Peggy Sue—the Buddy Holly Song.

Our house in the hills of Mill Valley was on a narrow winding road. If you met another car, the driver going downhill had to yield—put the car in reverse and back into somebody's driveway to allow the car going uphill to pass. Maybe that's why my parents bought the tiny Karmann Ghia.

It was a stick shift—a challenge driving in the San Francisco Bay Area with its steep hills, but a useful skill to have in life. I took my first driver's test in nearby Corte Madera. In those years the test required parallel parking. I'm embarrassed to say that it took me until the third try (my last chance) to successfully ma neuver into the space allotted, which could easily have accommodated a Mack truck. Parallel parking never got easier, and even today I'll drive blocks out of my way to avoid it. I somehow missed getting the parking gene.

* *

Fast-forward to the summer of 1968. My family had moved to

the Hollywood hills, buying a home in a new housing development just above the Lake Hollywood reservoir (where the movie *Chinatown* was filmed) and just under the H of the Hollywood sign. I had graduated from Hollywood High School, finished my first year at UC Santa Cruz (*Go, Banana Slugs!*) and was taking classes at UCLA during the summer quarter. That required driving the Karmann Ghia to the UCLA campus.

I carried my books in a large floppy basket with short leather handles. The road down to Barham Boulevard was a twisty one and as I took a curve one day, my basket of books flipped to the floor from the passenger seat. In my infinite wisdom, rather than stop the car or just let it be, I leaned over to grab the basket and grazed a retaining wall on my right, denting and scraping the front fender. Fortunately, I wasn't hurt, the body damage was minor, and the car was driveable.

I needed to get to class, so I decided to simply go on and deal with it later.

* *

One thing you need to know about me before I continue—I am rather compulsive about following rules. Give me some instructions and I will follow them to the letter. On the continuum of rule-followers, I probably rank in the 99th percentile. If a natural disaster struck the world and I was the only person left, I still wouldn't park in the handicap spot. But there's an exception to every rule, and this day was one.

I was pretty shaken and got more anxious on the long drive to UCLA. What would my father say? Maybe I could fix the situation, but how? As I neared the campus, I happened to pass an Earl Scheib paint and body shop. Earl Scheib's low-budget ads were on late-night tv all the time and this one was within walking distance of the campus. I could drop the car off, go to class, and maybe get it fixed in time to drive home later that day, right? That was my reasoning.

I had a checking account and went to the bank to withdraw cash. That way my father wouldn't see a cancelled check.

I don't remember what the cost was, but it wasn't horrible. To his credit the manager tried to talk me out of it. Wouldn't it be better to just level with my father? But I was panicked and insisted. He warned me that I really should leave it overnight—the paint would barely have time to dry properly and it might appear more matte than shiny. But I was determined and went ahead with it, driving home as late as I could—inventing some "library research" as I recall.

After that, I was in the driveway like a shot anytime the car needed washing, even though this was usually my younger brother's job. And I pulled it off for a couple of months. But one fateful Saturday, returning from errands with my mother, we pulled up to the house and I saw my brother in the driveway washing the Karmann Ghia. The jig was up. He had noticed the paint difference and some tell-tale baby blue drops on the chrome bumper. And told my father. Lying was uncharacteristic of me, so my father wasn't too harsh. He said the insurance would have paid for the damage, and that it was pretty dumb of me. Lesson learned.

* *

It was my brother who eventually totaled the Karmann Ghia, fortunately emerging unscathed. But for years—and I mean years—whenever we were driving and passed an Earl Scheib (and there were many of them), my brother or sister would never fail to casually comment, *"Oh look, Chris. There's an Earl Scheib."* Followed by silence, a conspiratorial smirk, and a suppressed giggle. You never live some things down.

Night Ride

by Cindi Pringle

body acquiesces
to gravity –
in a whirl
       rattled
tosses and turns
holds on
blurry figures
flash by
hair mussed
by thrust
distant squeals
       feign amusement

then
the empty side
of an edge
dips twice

must be the cat
       obscured
by darkness

it died a week ago

When I Was Closest to the Earth

by Cindi Pringle

Cool, moist, prickly shards of grass
    crumple under my youthful chest
lawn's sweetness fills nostrils with euphoria
my Gulliver's eye encounters
two ants stumbling up a tender, lime-green
    shoot toward the sun
Away from their Lilliputian
    civilization underground where
(thousands upon) millions
    of dutiful comrades till
loose soil, engorging
        Earth's placenta

My white canvas P.F. Flyers trundle
    where cars never would
over buckled concrete sidewalks
asphalt tennis courts laced with
    sticky black tar tentacles
up a gravel path, grinding stones underfoot
through scratchy thigh-high weedy fields
Hopscotch from rock to rock to rock to shore
    across the creek as it rambles
a piercing buzz of locusts crescendos
    overhead in trees' canopy
in humid afternoon heat

I was closest to the earth when
the tomato bush shimmies as I
    snap off fruits still warm
from the sun
A handful of wild blackberries
given up by brambles
along banks of the languid creek
    sours milk on cereal
sips off dainty red honeysuckle petals
    gift droplets of sugary nectar
to the tip of my tongue
curling with laughter

Still Life With Desk

by Janet Rendall

Wood. Primitive stuff. I hated natural products. Too high maintenance. Sleek chrome, glass and synthetic laminates were my preference. High tech furniture for a fast lane life. So how come I was in this consignment store? No clue.

I turned to escape when an old desk commanded my attention. Odd. Out of all the objects crammed into the jumbled space, this thing shoved back against a wall in the dim recesses of a corner drew me like a siren's call. Gray with dust and badly scarred, this would be a major time commitment. I glanced at my watch. Didn't I have somewhere to go?

"Are you interested in the desk, ma'am?" a man's voice asked— the store's owner, back again to pester me. Of course he would, I was his sole customer.

"Not really. The desk wouldn't fit with my other furnishings." I took a last look at the sagging frame that clutched its five drooping drawers. One of the knobs was gone. Maybe pulled off by impatient or inquisitive fingers?

Small explosions of life on or around this inanimate object had left their marks on it. Countless dings on the cellulose countenance were scabs that would never heal without the poultice of wood putty and sand paper. Even then, only the skill of an artisan woodworker could pull off that plastic surgery.

"This desk was fashioned as a wedding gift by the husband," he said, in the precise voice of a docent. "The desk's been in the same family for two generations. Notice these thumb-tack holes along the front?" He pointed to spots I could barely discern without my reading glasses. "They're from the Christmas stockings. You see, they had no fireplace, so the children created one by filling the knee-well space with crepe paper flames. I'm sure this piece has many tales to tell."

Great. That's all I needed. A talking desk with traumatic stress disorder. "You seem to know a lot about it."

"If you decide to purchase, I'll get more information from their daughter. Might be some wonderful stories here."

Weird. Did this guy know about my dry spell? My despair at facing perpetually blank pages? I shrugged and resumed my inspection. On the desk's left front corner "DK + SH" was carved into the wood, like a brand. Small teeth marks were visible on the lowest drawer pull and there were long scratches down one side panel, the cat no doubt. It didn't take a detective to deduce where the phone had resided. Doodles vined across the right rear corner and crept to the front, becoming more sophisticated as their journey progressed. A tiny peace symbol dangled at the doodle's terminus, almost down to the level of the pencil drawer.

Far back on the top, a great dark ink blotch added an air of mystery. My fingers trailed over the raised grain protruding from the blue-black splotch, hoping their sensitivity could ferret out the secrets it held. Maybe secrets so dark they would extinguish the light. That was only the writer in me, embellishing again. I ran a thumb over the ink spot, the whorls and knots beneath spoke of life-giving roots and branches that begged for a voice.

"I'll take it."

#

I circled the just delivered desk. What possessed me to buy this decrepit excuse for a writing surface? And, the bottom left drawer was stuck. After another forceful yank it pulled free so suddenly that a dusty "Clue-The Great Detective Game," dumped out onto the carpet. Printed on the upper left corner of the box: "First Edition,1949," Two antiques for the price of one. Cool. I hadn't played this game since the 1960s.

Like the desk, the scuffed game board, bent cards and grimy weapons had suffered through a tough life. I fingered the tiny rope, lead pipe, revolver, candlestick, knife and a wrench. How quaint. No assault rifle or a bomb in the mix. Nice.

The real crime here wasn't a murder, it was the mansion. The architect ought to be shot. No living room anywhere on the first floor? All space was taken by a ballroom, billiard room, study, conservatory, library, hall, lounge and kitchen. Sheesh. And to think I'd never questioned this absence of functionality back in the day. So much for a trip down memory lane—never what you expected. I closed the box.

A panel behind the drawer had come loose during the delivery, creating a gap through which a yellowed paper peeked. I teased out a postcard bearing a green one cent stamp postmarked Omaha, Neb, July 7, 1914 then risked a case of eye-strain to make out a name; Lilly Gamet? Address; Bonesteel, S.D. The cursive was excellent but almost impossible to read because it was written in pencil, faded and smudged to ghost-like graffiti. The gist of the message appeared to be driving instructions to an indecipherable location.

The flip side of the card consisted solely of a sepia toned photo—six children of various ages. A pretty teenager, big bows on her pigtails, held the youngest child, about ten-months-old. Intrigued, I consulted the internet. Bonesteel, South Dakota, laid out in 1902 and booming at the time, still existed as of 2010. Population: 275. Might be possible to find out who sent this card, if I was so inclined. I wasn't.

I pried off the panel with a screw-driver. Air-mail envelopes Par Avion, the kind with red and blue lines around the borders, spilled onto the rug. The letter on top of the heap was postmarked Manilla, Philippines, June 1, 1943. The one directly below, Los Angeles, 5:00 PM, April 7, 1944. Whoa. Better call the consignment store, that daughter would want these.

"The number you have reached is no longer in service," a robotic voice intoned with finality. How could that be? The desk had been delivered less than an hour ago. I re-dialed. Same result. My mouth went dry. The owner must have transposed one or two numbers. I bundled the letters into a grocery bag and took off.

Thirty minutes later I faced the store's dark windows. I put my face to the glass and stared in. Cobwebs glistened in the red light of an emergency exit sign. Huh? Except for cobwebs and dust bunnies the store was empty. I fought an urge to run and forced myself to survey the area. The store was on a corner, next to a weed infested vacant lot. A busy gas station occupied the space beside the store.

A dress store across the street had an unobstructed view of the consignment store so I walked over there to see if anyone inside knew anything.

The middle-aged saleswoman adjusted her glasses and glanced over my shoulder. "It closed about a year ago, not long after the owner died."

My palms were wet with sweat, my heart raced. Dizzy, I leaned against the jewelry case to remain vertical. Trying for something tangible I asked, "Were there any items left inside?"

The woman shrugged. "Not that I know of. The owner's son had everything carted away the day it closed."

I nodded, too stunned for a verbal response.

For the rest of the day, I obsessed over the desk's former owners and their relationship to the store. Now it was night, and my fingers inched toward the ink splotch, drawn to it by the gravity of the black hole. Nonsense, my thumb reminded me, there is no hole. The hair on my arm stood up, pointing at the dark spot. Static electricity? No, a definite electrical pull. Deep breath. Calm down. I was spooking myself.

To occupy mind and hands, I sorted the letters and inspected their postmarks. They ranged geographically from San Francisco and Los Angeles, to the New Hebrides and the Philippines. Two from London. All delivered between 1942 and 1945. Every one of them had been opened, then meticulously taped closed. An aura of foreboding encompassed them.

I reached for a stack of Air Mail letters, tied with a black satin ribbon. All postmarked from 1960 to 1965, every one of them stamped PRAY FOR PEACE. Well, that hadn't worked. So many Peace Protests. Classmates in body bags. MIAs, POWs. More lost later, from PTSD, Agent Orange, and Napalm exposure. Later still, personally selected chemicals taken to block the pain. My fingers disobeyed my brain and returned to the desk top to trace an ink thread on its circuitous route to the peace symbol. A pang of regret shot through my heart. I dropped the letters. Couldn't go there.

My fingers slid away from the peace symbol and crept back to the ink splotch. The raised wood grains, coarse at first, had inexplicably softened. My index finger disappeared into it, up to the second knuckle. Impossible. This must be a dream.

Cold. Freezing cold. My hand and arm had numbed and the magnetic draw on my finger was so intense that sudden suction jerked me off balance. I fell headlong onto the desk. Splinters stabbed my shoulder, wood particles ground into tender facial skin. I stopped struggling. Resistance would hurt more.

All silent. All dark. Not a breath of movement. Not a whiff of odor.

Where was I?

An unreadable slat of wood—maybe a sign—hung suspended in the mist and a form emerged in this gray world. It displayed a distinct walking pattern and a familiar tilt of the head. I was face to face with—myself? If so, a cowl had fallen away. I had 20/20 vision—perception so clear it was hindsight, not foresight. Had I passed on?

That couldn't be—I was in the desk. Gut cramping—perspiring—fighting the claustrophobia of the boxed in. How could I be alive? Tears. Made perfect sense. Tears stored for decades, had poured into the ink splotch and turned it into a well. I could either swim out between cellulose strands or disappear for one hundred years, like the entire Scottish village of Brigadoon.

Too weary to go on, I whispered, "Go ahead, take me."

The ink obliged.

I swam on a current of electricity. Juiced. Alive and free—improbable. I was trapped inside a block of furniture while experiencing the cumulative traumas of its life. Losses of family, friends, pets, health. Ambiguous losses too; hopes and dreams.

"I don't want to own this thing!" If my voice made a sound, it disappeared into the void a few seconds before echoing back. *Half a century ago, you were the one who tattooed the desk's face. The one who transferred possession of it to the consignment store but never gave up ownership. Part of you remained in the desk and it in you.*

Laughing Boy

by Kate Feinberg Robins

My toddler is trying to make me feel better
and I love him so much for it.
He turns on the fan and sees me smile and says,
"Are you funny?"
and laughs
and does it again.

The Last Diaper

BY KATE FEINBERG ROBINS

Sitting on the floor,
knees curled up,
back against the wall,
I write furiously
and sob.

My almost-4-year-old
looks up,
comes near,
wraps small arms around me.

Melting into each other,
chests rising and falling,
tears dampening a head of dark curls,
I gently pull back
and look into his eyes.

Steadily, firmly, in the languages we know best, I explain:

> *No se dice* "No thank you" *al hacer pichi.*
> *O te sientas en el* potty *o te cambias tu pañal.*
> *No es aceptable decir* "No thank you."
> *Estoy harta.*

> You don't say, "No thank you" to peeing.
> Either you sit on the potty or you change your own diaper.
> You can't just say, "No thank you."
> I'm done.

After lunch, I watch silently
as he walks into the bathroom,
sits on the potty,
pees,
wipes,
washes his hands.

"*¿Estás listo?*" I ask him. – Are you ready? –

He looks me in the eye
and says, "*Sí.*"

"My" Golden Girls: The Impact of Unexpected Connections

BY LESLIE ROUNDY

I always had a special bond with my mother. The youngest of four children, naturally my siblings referred to me as "the spoiled one." I prefer to think of myself as "the chosen one." My parents didn't plan on having another child after the premature birth of my twin sisters, and if I recall correctly, Mom was advised not to have more children. Keep in mind that this was in the early 1950s, and medical innovations were nothing like they are today. Yet seven years later, I arrived on a Monday morning, the day after Mother's Day.

Fast forward to adulthood. My mom and I remained close, not always in miles but always in our hearts. A few years after my father passed away, my siblings and I decided it was time for Mom to live with me—the chosen one. She was in her 80s, and although she was still getting along ok, we knew it was the best decision for her safety and well-being.

I often struggled with determining what my life's purpose was. I knew it wasn't to have a family of my own or to climb the pro-verbial corporate ladder. I don't remember how long Mom had been living with me when suddenly one day it became crystal clear. I indeed *was* the chosen one. I truly believe God put me on this earth to take care of Mom when the time came, and I wouldn't have had it any other way. She was my purpose.

I began to notice that Mom was having "senior moments" more often. I chalked them up to the normal aging process. It wasn't until we returned from a trip that I realized how quickly her memory was declining. One evening she came out of her bed-room and asked, "Leslie, where *are* we?" It struck me as odd, but I attributed it to the long drive home. The incidents continued—some more severe than others—and as a family we eventually made the difficult decision to move Mom into a memory care facility.

It was an incredibly hard time, especially in the beginning. As the months passed, Mom and I both began to adjust in our own way, and this new way of living became more familiar—the daily routines, the surroundings, the staff. During my visits with Mom, I also started to get to know the residents, either through interactions in the activities room or during a meal.

There were a few women in particular that I established closer bonds with over time. "My" Golden Girls were nothing like Blanche, Dorothy, Rose, and Sophia of the 1980s sitcom. They didn't always make sense when they talked and they exhibited odd behaviors at times, but I loved being around them.

The first one I got to know was Tammy. She was the sweetest little lady and Mom's best friend. Whenever I greeted her, she would say, "It's so nice to see you." Mom missed her cat Tyger dearly, so I would sometimes show her and the other ladies at the dining table pictures of him. Tammy always asked, "How many cats do you have?" and when I answered three, she got a surprised look on her face and repeated in disbelief "Three?!" We had that conversation every time I showed pictures of my cats. Tammy didn't talk a lot, although we did have a long chat one day during which she told me all about her family. I learned that she met her husband in Maryland, has a son in Texas, liked cream and sugar in her coffee, and loved sushi. When my visit was over and I stood up to leave, she would take my hand and say, "It was so nice to see you." I would carry that joyful sentiment with me throughout the day.

And then there was Rosemary. Where to start. She was my comedian. One day during a visit, it came time to move from the activities room into the dining room. After getting Mom situated with her walker, I was helping Rosemary get hers. Mom was standing next to her, and she pretended to reach into Mom's sweater pocket. She said with great excitement, "Oh, five hundred dollars!" and "put" it in her pocket. I had to look away because I didn't want her to see me chuckling. A few weeks later, Rosemary looked down at my shoes—nothing fancy, plain ol' black sandals—and said, "Oh, I love your shoes. (Long pause.) I'm going to steal those tonight!" And then she flashed me that big, wide grin I had become accustomed to.

Last but not least was Eleanor, a sweet little lady who always wore a button-down sweater and was never seen without perfectly styled hair. She rarely made sense and spoke very softly, but that didn't deter me from interacting with her. One night at dinner I noticed Eleanor had a blue folder with her, and I asked her what was in it. She slowly opened it, and inside were four pieces of paper. She started turning them over. Each one was the same—a drawing of a simple tie, like what you would see in a child's coloring book. The pages were a little worn, with a little food on them, but they were hers, and she was being very protective of them. The last time I saw Eleanor that night, she was walking through the courtyard, headed to a different resident cottage, carrying her folder, a cloth napkin, and one of the trays from the dining table that holds sugar. G'night Eleanor.

I felt a sense of purpose whenever I was around those special ladies, whether it was opening a package of crackers for them or helping them put together a puzzle. Don't get me wrong, Mom was still my purpose, my number one purpose. She always would be. But I knew I could give a little to the other residents, too. One thing I learned: all they wanted was for someone to talk to them and treat them like a normal person—the person they were before their memory began to fail them and their world was turned upside down. Some five years later, I'm still feeling the impact that those interactions had on me. It gave me such joy knowing that I helped others and brightened their day, even if they wouldn't remember it a short time later. I received so much more than I gave, and for that I am grateful.

Brake Lights Ahead

BY PATRICIA L. SCRUGGS

Street signs vanish.
And behind every lamp post,
a dark shape.

The rain has come at last.
Relief from the drought.

Soft at first,
then hard, then harder.

It drums on the tight skins of roofs.
Hail beats on skylights.

The deluge fills gutters,
floods streets.

Driving, I keep my speed low,
watch the brake lights ahead.

Plumes of water thrown up by trucks
blot out white lines on the road.

Monogamy Among Males

BY PATRICIA L. SCRUGGS

mosquito, they mate, then die
Peru poison frog
black vulture
prairie vole
Malagasy jumping rat

cockroach, there's a surprise

nine species of birds of paradise
bald eagle
grey wolf
Kirks dik dik
penguin: African, Megellanic, Gentoo and Royal

Schistosoma mansoni, that parasitic worm

wood duck
shingleback skink, the bulkiest of the blue tongues
albatross
titi monkey
Cape spurfowl

some think
swans
Canada geese
gibbons
but they have been known
to take more than one mate
in the same season

my husband cuts flowers from the garden
arranges them in a vase on the table

To My Older Brother: Reasons Why You Should Not Make Me Executor of Your Will

-After Mindy Mettafee

by Patricia L. Scruggs

1. Until you were six, we were best friends. Then you started school and discovered that you weren't supposed to like girls. I became dirt to you. I am still a girl.

2. We hid behind the sofa in that motel we stayed at in Calgary while Dad looked for a house for us. It was our cave and we were bears hibernating through the winter. Are you sure you want a bear to distribute your estate?

3. If it involves math, you need to find someone else. When we were in second and third grades in the same room, Miss Bishop called the second graders to the blackboard. I was doing my arithmetic thinking how those pushy sevens look like geese. I joined the others too late. Miss Bishop made me walk to the cloakroom. She followed with the black strap from her desk drawer. I refused to hold out my hands for her, so she hit me on the arm. You made fun of me later, but you didn't tell Mom.

4. Remember that time you and your friends chased me up a tree and threw firecrackers at my bare legs? Do you really want someone who is not a fighter? Although, when you called me skinny, I threw a wet dishrag at you. It hit you in the face. Thank you for not killing me then.

5. I can be sneaky. I'm the one who drew mustaches on the Vargas pinups you lined your walls with. You never seemed to notice. Did you even look at their faces?

6. Thank you too, for messing up, so I wouldn't have to. You

quit high school. Stole a carton of cigarettes and ended up arrested. Worked as a fire spotter for the forestry service. Joined the army. Got stationed in Hawaii, not Europe where you wanted to go. Showed them, never left the base. Married the wrong girl because you were lonely. Got divorced. Married the right girl, but she died in a car accident leaving you to raise three teenagers. I hope they are in the will.

7. You threatened to beat Don up after we started dating. But when I married him three years later, you gave me away. Then you cried at the end of the ceremony.

8. What if I die first?

9. I don't want either one of us to die.

Waiting for News of the Operation

BY PATRICIA L. SCRUGGS

Dust motes quiver in the slant
of afternoon sun.

A hanging prism breaks
a rainbow against the wall.

Through the study window the stoplight
now green now yellow now red.

Nightfall, lights switch on
in surrounding houses.

A sickle moon rises
through menacing clouds.

What's said. What's not
said in the dark,

as if street sounds
could silence our stillness

while we wait.
Wait for the scream

of the telephone.

Cookies

BY KRISTINE ANN SHELL

Everyone talks about the convenience of online shopping. If you follow the talk, you'll be told that online shopping is superior to mall shopping, and that online shopping will eliminate the need for retail stores and shopping malls.

The pandemic forced me to shop online. Shopping at retail stores and malls, even with COVID-19 restrictions lifted, remains difficult. So, I've been shopping online. Enjoying the speed and convenience of online shopping.

But online shopping isn't all speed and convenience. I've noticed that every time I start browsing online, I'm offered cookies. And, while I appreciate the offers, I never check the box that says I will accept the cookies. Still, the cookies find their way to my computer screen, uninvited. So, the shoes I was shopping for last week, online, are still stalking me this morning. In fact, the minute I'm on the internet, my computer screen is filled with ads for shoes. And not just any shoes, but strappy sandals that look very similar to the shoes I bought online. I want to tell someone that I already bought my sandals, and those sandals are on their way to my home. But there's no one to tell. So, I'm forced to look at all these ads for strappy sandals that look like the ones I just bought.

So, those cookies! I know they're tracking me, watching me, spying on me. And they are not benign. They're armed with Artificial Intelligence and constantly changing algorithms that know me better than I know myself. And who knows if those third-party cookies are selling my private information to some murky data brokers, because I don't own my personal information and personal data once the cookies grab it.

Beautiful Brown – Lovely Ladies

BY CAROLYN L. SNOW

● Elegant brown skinned women
Seamstresses, chefs, bakers
Strong yet silent
Fierce yet meek
Resourceful
Easy smile
A lady
● Exquisitely dressed
Tailored sophisticated suits, chic dresses, pillbox hats
Delicate gloves
Sporting elegant patent pocketbooks
Adorned in lovely hats
Beautiful dresses
Elegant browned skinned women
Daytime, maids, cooks, chefs
● Tailors, Teachers, Medicine Women
Strong hands
Easy smile
Country doctors
Creating, toting, giving elixirs and cures
Powerful yet dainty
Brilliant yet uneducated
Ficrcc yct mcck
● Moms, Aunties, Cousins, Wives, Friends
Elegant browned skinned women
● Five-star bakers
Master chefs with meager ingredients
Flour, butter, cream, sugar, eggs, vanilla…birthday cakes,
wedding cakes, funeral cakes, church cakes, pound cakes,
picnic cakes, ice cream

- Grand Mothers, Great Grand Mothers, daytime Maids, Cooks, Chefs, Nannies
  Church mothers, deaconesses, mentors, Pastor's wives
  Confidants, Heroes, Shelter
  a strong tower, a covering…mentors
  the backbone of the black family
- Mediators
  defender of the meek
  terror for the strong
  A listening ear
  Giving, caring, loving, sharing
  Graceful manners
  Comforting smile
- Lovely
  Beautiful brown Ladies
  A comfortable place called strength love and care

Untitled

by David Stone

"I bet this is a conspiracy," you said as you passed the bag of Beyond Meat 8-piece combos to your daughter. "Get a picture of that sign, Kay. There's no reason we should still be experiencing a national coin shortage after more than two years of this pandemic."

Boo-dup.

"Dad, your phone's recording you."

"What?"

"That was Siri, Dad. You're being recorded."

"Don't be a fool. Put that phone down and pay attention to our drinks so they don't spill."

"You're the fool, Dad."

The lights of a high profile vehicle pulling closer to the rear of your family's van highlighting your head should have made you trust your daughter's instincts, but you continued to talk, scanning the light in front of you, the one-eyed glare in your side mirror, and the double-eyed beams in your rearview mirror.

"Dad, why are you nervous?" Kay asked.

"Looks like we're being followed. You must have been right about the phone," you insisted as you turned abruptly.

The fruit punch and Diet Coke tilted in the paper cup holder on the floor.

"Look out, Dad! You're the one who's going to spill the drinks."

Boo-dup.

"What was that, Kay?"

"I told you, Dad, that's Siri."

At that point you scanned your mirrors again. Still one-eye in the left mirror and two in the rear. You stayed straight on the same street as you lightly poked Kay in the arm and pointed at the phone. Furrowing your brows, you swiped the finger on your hand closest to your phone to indicate that Kay should power it off.

Kay raised her eyebrows and pointed at the phone, seeming to search for confirmation that you wanted your phone turned off.

Rapidly looking from the windshield, to the mirrors, to Kay, you emphatically nod your head yes.

Kay did what you asked and shut down the phone. The lights in the mirrors suddenly fell back. The distance grew between you and the vehicle behind you.

"Looks like a black van. I don't see any markings. Looks like they're going to leave us alone, Kay."

Boo-dup.

"You might want to thank this kind woman who was following you for calling in your accident. She's the reason we got here so quickly," said a police officer, just coming into focus for you. He appears confused. You could see him looking around with as much confusion as yourself. "Well, it looks like she's gone, Sir."

"You grabbed the phone and attempted to throw it out the window, just missing your daughter's head. The phone bounced off the window and hit you in your head, Sir. Your van swerved and ran over the curb and into this stone wall. Your vehicle's airbags inflated. You and your daughter are going to have some significant bruising, and it looks like you are going to have one enormous goose egg from where your phone hit you, but you're both going to be okay," said the paramedic leaning over.

"Dad, she used your phone to call for help. She left it with me. Don't worry, Dad. It's still working, but super sus, Dad, your Siri no longer has the voice of a woman. When I asked Siri to call Mom, a man's voice replied."

Kay looks around. "It sounds just like the police officer, Dad. The one who was just here, but he's gone."

Dreamers

by Heather Takenaga

I want the house,
    I want the expertise,
I want the spouse,
    I want the title,
        I want the community—
   rights
          of a
      h u m a n
   r e g i s t e r e d   to
      w o r k - - - c a r e e r - - - - - - - - - life

I want the stars,
    I want the moon,
  I want Mars,
     I want the sunshine,
        I want silence—
   flights
 of a
s o u l
    f l o a t i n g
          in   d r e a m s

Desires spoken, wishes deaf
  Strawberry-puckered eyes to coffee-licked nights
    What planet are we on
      that our two lives should collide?
    How can we survive
     together

  when our life waters
    d r y
      O u t ?

Mornings with Jojo

by Heather Takenaga

"You know, I cough up hairballs better than that garbage you feed me! That's why I don't eat."

I look at Jojo and gaze into his sleep-riddled blue eyes. Then I scratch his head. While he purrs and rolls onto my hand, crushing it with all eleven pounds of his silver fluff, I kiss my little prince on his gray-striped crown. His white whiskers slice into my cheek while we snuggle closer to one another.

"And your breath stinks, hoonam."

I nuzzle his face so his wet pink nose brushes against mine. I love how I can get away with it. Against my ear is his soft drumming of life. He repays me by rolling his bony shoulders into my knuckles. My fingers aren't supposed to bend that way. I keep trying to scratch anyways.

"Don't stay up so late looking at that light thing again. You took too long! Tsk-tsk!"

I wiggle my other arm free from the covers to poke at Jojo's striped paws. When we got him, he was already declawed. Poor thing. I'd want to feel how sharp he'd cling to me. I poke at his jellybean pads instead, a spotted mix of pink and violet. Every paw is a different pattern. His Grace permits me to touch each one without flinching.

"Remember, hoonam, we sleep together. To.get.her! We're on a tight schedule here."

I bury my nose into his pearly pudge. Jojo has the softest fur, semi-long and somehow never tangled. He takes good care of himself. He always smells like sunshine. His smokey tail thumps hard on the mattress when I start humming into him, the only warning sign to his mighty squeaky roar.

"Time for food, hoonam. Jojo needs his rest!"

Ah, Jojo. He knows. He's so demanding. And, as always, so smart.

When I raise my head, my stomach rumbles. My hair is tangled underneath me. Pillow is squished. The cover is mangled. Sunlight is blazing white from the blinds. My nose is running. I feel cold all over.

I get up and start my day.

Box in the Green Corner

BY HEATHER TAKENAGA

Across concrete borderlines,
they lived among
orange blossoms and Buddhist shrines
since they were young,
hopping from floors of red dirts
to linoleum and fur rugs,
closets of silk suits and shirts,
sparkling glasses and coffee mugs.

No matter the household
of his and hers,
stashes of silver and gold
unseen for years,
but closer within are traces
of letters, slides, Polaroid clips—
so many faces, faces, faces!
Shots of blank lips
for those who remain.

They rest in a giant cardboard box,
next to their worn walking canes
and countless ticking clocks.
Someday
they would tell us,
they said, they
would discuss
how and why and where to send
those souls froze in pose.

In the end
silence was what they chose.

Ah, what richness they give
under blankets of dust
to live,
to entrust
stories from the green corner,
our assorted, mute mourner.

3:14 AM

BY HEATHER TAKENAGA

I'm not ready to say goodbye
to the ancient fire.
I'm not ready to say goodbye
to the ancient fire.

She warms me,
she fosters me,
she lights me up.
She rests on
the pedestal of a goddess.

Without the blacks of memories
the fire dims.

Without the whites of medicine
the fire sputters.

Yet as each day passes
the fire devours,
the fire reaches.

Let it roar.
Do not extinguish it.
Flare up the night.
Keep the fire bright.

I'm not ready to say goodbye
to the ancient fire.
I'm not ready to say goodbye
to the ancient fire.

Summer Slumber

BY HEATHER TAKENAGA

Harvest moon,
were it not for you,
how could I end summer?
You are the beacon for
gray days, lantern nights,
the calling of scarlet hills
and aging maple trees.

Harvest moon,
how many lovers
gazed at your
rays, dipped in twilight but
unable to hide,
they instead bask in
your beauty?

Harvest moon,
how many souls
have passed by your
watchful eye, in their march
towards their place in the
heavens? Do you greet them,
curse them?

I sing to you,
harvest moon,
before your golden sister
consumes you. You bring
us majesty in this blackness,
you tell us it is fit to rest.

Dance of Delirium

by Elizabeth Uter

The ancients used to say
there is a dance of ecstasy,
of rapture so profound
that in the thrashing of movements
all is lost to madness — eyes rolling in
the head — it's the sort of extreme
when bodies whirling are beyond beyond.
 Spiritual dervishing — the turn, the turns
— it's as if possessed.
Sometimes not even following steps.
They are moving in delirium,
abandoning self to eternal and
internal rhythm leading to trance.
Sacred dancing to the god Dionysus,
he who liberated wine and as if in
drunken stupor, his followers, Maenads,
maidens all demand that no man must
watch as they flow, flop and drop
 and if male eyes see their ways,
they would tear him limb from limb
— could not suffer him to live.
Where do these wild ones
go behind the blankness of eye?
It is said they wait in a transcendent
state within the mind of their god.

Museum at World's End

BY ELIZABETH UTER

The museum at the end of the world reopens for business.
It has mechanised legs that walk its bulk about the yard.
Some say it looks a like a hairy millipede stretching
aching feet in a dance across a sun-bleached patch.
Inside as strange as outside, it contains
the secret things of our planet — imagine all the thoughts
of every single soul trapped in amber-like vessels each
receiving, giving off silky vapours in different shades
— black, white, gold, red, umber, silver — a continuous
coiling in and out — is the sinewing of snaky shapes.
There are blessings, curses to-ing and fro-ing.
There are heartstrings dangling from ceilings
emoting notes as if from golden harps.

There are words that make up the walls, *sturdy,*
weak, beautiful, harsh, meek, combining to form
a solid whole. Then there is The Curator, a raggedy man,
as if formed from the parts of a puzzle, sky-blue here,
cloud puffs there … blank … blank … green tree,
chrysanthemums there — a painted horse-head on
his coat front, a badger on his back, a hat the size
 of a chimney stack with giraffe designs overlaying that
— ever sliding downwards. His face a mystery — eyes
peridot-deep gems, nose as straight as eagles'
wings and rounded mouth full of fluff
— it's the stuffing that makes up a plush toy.
He's a clockwork invention. Precise at stacking
shelves, stamping approval on items to be removed.
The museum at world's end is opening today and
the strange things of life will come alive at once and play.

Over the Edge

BY ELIZABETH UTER

Over the edge of the world
— it must have been a little like this
for the early explorers
— a scrap of a map the *Imago Mundi*,
a Babylonian treasure
or the full scope and measure of
The *Piri Reis* showing Africa,
Europe, Brazil in times before history
says they should've been shown or known
by the Ottoman Empire. The world on fire
with the want, the need, the greed
the speed to know more and more,
see more, be more, have more.
A universe of abundance
must have felt like
their flat-packed world
— as detailed as an idea from IKEA
— would slip them into oblivion or
the abyss, off the edge of the world
— scenario in book folio, quarto, octavio
— a waterfall lip that could lead
to Valhalla, the glory port of berserkers
or a Christian Hell that housed the shells
of men, of women — innumerable
as the breath of every human then and now
glimpsed over all past ages into one drop.
Travelling to the end of the ends

of the earth could be the birth of

extraordinary life on terra, to

know that you on your

Island are not alone if

you just peeped

— is how we feel about the universe

today, wishing to

traverse space, time.

Continually chasing how far thoughts

made manifest can lead us

— boldly going in this form

where no man has gone before.

To know who we are, where we

 are right now and where we need to go.

The Quantum Undead

BY ELIZABETH UTER

I gnaw at the neck of my daily bread,
blood oozing, nurturing, sucking
as a baby does, leaving my mark as bites
that give life until I am all-Vampire,
undead, untiring, capable of feats too strange
to be believed — flying through ether as far
as the cosmos can ken — touching ice-cold tails
of fiery comets — dangling from stars
— approaching black holes with some
foreboding, I admit - turning back when
I feel the tiniest tug, the pull of a predator
better than me at consuming.
Remembering the saying:
'if your hand is in the tiger's mouth,
take it out slowly, carefully.'
Withdrawing with caution
from difficulty achieved
without sleeve, suit or ship.

My natural bent is for travel,
barely alighting on the human
plane — they complain too much
always wah-wahing, sally-moaning
about things of slight consequence.
Science once said *they are 5 minutes
from midnight* — the other day these same
lame cynics crawled out of

the cracks of their scientific labs to
whisper 'today it's now 90 seconds away.'
The Doomsday Clock measuring
how close to global calamity and insanity
— moments from the zero hour they are
full of fun facts and fatuous acts.
Truth is, I don't have to stay in one
dimension. I am cosmic, quantum,
ghoulish, after all. A bloodsucking bug
drifting high on celestial zephyrs
— keeping safe by using the brain I've acquired
through eating, through seeking the necks of the best.

The Stairs at the End

by Elizabeth Uter

I glance around grand on this high stair.
A cooling chair, looking down
with temperatures decreasing.
Darkened sky, colours less intense
— once vibrant greens, splashes
of flower-red, yellow-orange, pink
— now as glass — slippery but clear
in the fading light.
'Pearlescent,' slips from my lips,
I play with the word. I feel like
a shell on a beach in the tropics,
lustre of psychedelic day
dissipates into endless twilight-grey,
snapping into midnight-black.

As I wait for the bus on this step
at the end of the world, I wrap
my lightweight, cream-coloured
cardigan tight about me, pearl-shaped
buttons not enough to stave off the cold.
How is it possible, this once tropical
moment has turned to ice so fast?
My brother a blur beside me says
throughout the day, 'we have steadily
been moving closer to *the gods,*'
Oops! My slip, 'the mountains.'

With the loss of light comes a chill
in the bones — you cannot believe.
I did not expect to be here so late
— missed connections — opportunities
slipping like dew from late flowering
blooms in the dark and now this stop.
I sniff, my dress *so* thin A4 paper
could slap it about and still stand tall.

People retiring from the market, wandering
in slow motion, toe to red earth, up then down,
healing to the moment as they circle,
waiting for transport. No timetable stamped
to the door of the closed station office
but there is a knowing in the sky; the trees
leaning in; leaves are fingers whispering
that time's immaterial here. When the bus comes
it comes, it is always this way.
Christiana, JA's a pretty place, a lovely name
— not as drafty as a U.K.'s pseudo-summer's day
but here when every day is 30°C,
an unexpected drop at night by 15° will separate
the stoics from the scaredy-cats, I am that cat.
I am loitering on a stone throne, aching.
The bus in the longness of night will come.

When Pablo Met Marina

BY GUDELIA "DELIA" VADEN

I gathered bits and pieces of these faded memories from my family. It was not easy, as many have since passed away. My story is about how Pablo first met Marina, at a time so long ago. The story of how my grandparents first met has more differences than similarities than when I first met my husband, Tom. The differences were mainly due to the women not having the educational opportunities that women of today have, such as they did not go to school. It was also believed that a woman's place was in the home.

When I met Tom at the ice cream vending machine at Merced College, the newly created campus was bursting with students. It was easy to tell Tom was a math major, as he was never without his slide rule that he carried in a leather pouch. At nineteen, I am not positive whether it was his intellect or his emerald green eyes, but boy did I fall head over heels! It was love at first sight.

In 1898, it was not even summer yet in Jerez, Zacatecas, as Marina was wiping her brow with a handkerchief. She looked up and noticed a young man on a gold-colored palomino. His steel blue eyes, dimpled chin and chiseled jaw made her heart skip a beat. Marina thought she had died and gone to heaven. Why else would she meet such a handsome knight on a horse! She was picking nopales (cactus) for her mom; it was the young and tender ones that were best for eating. In the process, Marina had pricked her finger and let out a big screech, "aye, aye, aye"!

Pablo, at eighteen, looked down from his horse and noticed Marina, who with her long brown braids resembled a child more than a young lady of fourteen. After inquiring in his Castilian accent if she was alright, he realized he would like to marry her. She did admit that he sounded funny in his way of talking that was so different from the way her family spoke. My grandmother told me that after Pablo and his family came to Mexico from Madrid Spain, he never lost his accent. She loved him regardless of how he spoke.

He wasted no time in asking Marina's father for her hand in marriage. He promised her father that he would provide and love her for the rest of his life, if only he would give them his blessing. Pablo gave her father a team of oxen, cows, horses and land as a wedding gift.

The modest family was pleased with Pablo's generosity. Marina's mom did warn her that vaqueros (cowboys) tended to love their horse more than their wife. It was just yesterday that she quit playing with dolls. Marina felt her heart beating with joy at the thought of marrying Pablo. She knew that she had followed Mexican tradition to marry young, and that since she was the oldest, she would be first to marry. Her mother had not only taught her to cook, but embroider and sew as well. She made her wedding dress of cotton and embroidered flowers. It was common for girls that were pure, such as Marina, to marry in a white dress. Her bouquet consisted of light pink dahlias and white carnations. She favored dahlias, the national flower of Mexico.

Pablo and Marina got married on a scorching hot summer day at Sanctuario de Nuestra Senora de la Soledad (Soledad Sanctuary) Catholic church in Jerez, Zacatecas, with its stained glass windows and statues of our Lord and his mother, Mary. I am positive that if the statues could talk, they would wish them well. There were 300 guests smiling and laughing from ear to ear. The reception was held at the hacienda Pablo shared with his parents. The mariachis played a couple of corridos and other familiar songs, such as Tengo el Alma Enamorada, among the gardens and fountains. The planting beds were bursting with pink dahlias, white lilies and red roses that adorned the metal arches. To this day the foods of the celebration makes my mouth water just thinking about how appetizing it was. The roasted pork, carne asada, poblano peppers, enchiladas, and a table with all kinds of juicy fruits such as purple grapes from their vineyards, golden peaches, and lime green guavas. Wines and horchata were the drinks of choice, and of course, tequila.

Pablo and Marina loved each other very much and stayed married. They had seven children. Their children were their pride and joy. My father, Vicente, was their middle child. Marina's mother was wrong as Pablo loved Marina even more than his beloved horse.

I learned that I am the woman I am today because my grandparents gave me a rich heritage of Mexican and Spanish culture. They also gave me morals, values and traditions that I will cherish for as long as I live. They may be gone, but I will value their legacy, for it is part of my heritage. This is all that is known about how Pablo met Marina.

The Proposal

by Gudelia "Delia" Vaden

I never imagined that I would receive a proposal, especially since I was already married. Tom and I got married in January of 1966. Just a year later and to our delight, our daughter, Natalie, was born in Orlando, Florida. We took one look at her big brown eyes and we were in love. We lived in a light beige house, the color of sand, not too far from Mc Coy AFB, where my husband, Tom was employed as an electronic technician. Life was great! Each day we would take romantic strolls on the beach with baby tucked into a bright red stroller, and in the evening we would view the sun-set painting hues of gold and crimson.

Our happy life was soon disrupted as Tom received orders to be deployed to Guam. My mind was at a blank as tears were running down my cheeks. Why Guam! Where the hell is Guam! Tom met with the base commander, as he asked if family could go. He was very firm in his decision and it was a flat no! The reason being that Guam was no place for a baby. The following week, after numerous kisses and long embraces, Tom boarded a plane and headed for Guam. I felt like I was losing it and could not stop crying, but knew I had to get it together as I had my baby daughter of six weeks and I had to be strong for her.

Should I stay or leave Orlando, Florida? That seemed to be the big question so far. The Orlando Sentinel would report stories of various crimes including rapes in our hometown. I decided to call my parents and see what they had to say. My dad spoke first and told me to pack my things and stay with them for a while, at least until Tom returned from his deployment. He also mentioned that he had built a guest room and had added a white crib. I was grateful for my parents' generosity and the living expenses my husband sent. We would be barely making it.

Four out of my seven siblings lived at home in Planada, not too far from Merced, California. Manuel lived in Le Grand, while Paul lived in Fremont, and Socorro, my eldest sister, lived in Los Banos. She was a teacher who married a millionaire, Dominic, who owned a dairy. They had just built a large family room for entertaining, birthday parties, baptisms and whatever. Italian families love to have parties with plenty of food. Dominic was a fantastic cook and just thinking about his spaghetti makes my mouth water. There was usually a dozen or so people at their family functions and I enjoyed meeting and sharing a meal with them.

On this particular day, it was Dominic's Aunt Sally's birthday and Socorro kept getting distracted and talking with Dominic's cousin, Antonio. I never got into the conversation and knew nothing about what was being discussed. Socorro later told me that Antonio wanted to get to know me. All I could say was what, what exactly are you talking about! We do not know each other. All I knew was what my sister told me; that he was rich, lived with his mother, and was about thirty. I thought that this can't be real. This only happens in the movies!

During a summer get together, Antonio's dark blue eyes met mine. He had a dozen red roses with white babies breath and was on one knee, asking me to marry him. He mentioned that he was a millionaire and he could provide a comfortable life for baby and me. I had to turn him down, reason being that I was already married and waiting for my husband to return from Guam. That I would wait however long it took for him to come home. That I loved him more than anything. My mind was made up and all his pleading did not do any good.

Remembering this time in my life, I surprised myself that at twenty-three, I was mature. And, that I could not be enticed by money or material things!

Point of View

by Thomas Vaden

Leaves falling
Grand pallet of puzzling color
Red, brown, blue hues mixed in a hodgepodge of mystery.
Why so beautiful are the leaves trampled over with little notice?
Why did I pause and take a picture of this inconspicuous tapestry?
Why do I remember this? Where was I?

At the base of Yosemite Falls
All are Looking up!
And, I am looking down?
The sky a perfect blue with water cascading down cliffs
Dancing around rocks glistening in the sun.
All are amazed; all are taking in the grandeur.

And, I am staring at the ground?
Why did I, at this moment in time, observe what others do not see?
Alone in my thoughts, I am unrestrained by all that nature offers!

Do I see things differently?

An Ode to a Marine

we will miss you; we will always love you

BY THOMAS VADEN

I knew a man, a son and brother
Who drowned in combat maneuvers
Preparing for a Satanic war.

A man not entombed on the Vietnam wall
Not recognized for his sacrifices to all.
A simple tombstone marks the grave
Of a marine, a brother so brave.

Patrick Leo Vaden, born on May 2, 1944 in St. Louis, Missouri
He withdrew from Mercy High School in September of 1961 to join the Marine Corp
He died in Okinawa on June 6, 1962

From Leader of the Pack to a Happy Camper

by Thomas Vaden

In the past, my freedom was limited to helping others succeed in their work. I often led groups of auditors, accountants and other statisticians in comprehensive studies designed to find ways to improve the internal operations of the Air Force. And, the rewards came from the accolades received about a job well done. I liked my job as a chief statistician, but now it has been relegated to the past. I am no longer the "leader of the pack."

Now, I am retired and free to do whatever. But what do I do with my newfound freedom? My wife, Delia, introduced me to line dancing, dragging me out of the house to try something new. She said "You are not going to sit at home and watch TV!" Thus, I had to learn how to do things that I have never tried before, and share my new adventures with others. Line dancing is such an adventure which, if accomplished well, provides avenues of joy previously unexplored. We took classes at the Janet Goeske senior center, and became quite good at line dancing. I have even performed at local senior centers, the Riverside Convention Center and the LA County Fair.

Delia also commented that it would be fun to paint with watercolors. She invited me to join her in this endeavor. Delia knew of my love of elephants and suggested I paint one. I did just that. Today the painting is displayed on the wall of our family room. Family members comment on the rich green, brown and golden hues of my painting, thus adding a unique dimension to my elephant. My heart swells with pride upon hearing these compliments.

I thought I had heard it all and that Delia and I were through exploring things to do upon retirement, but guess what? She got me interested in writing. Though, not at first. I had never written too much about things, unless they were government documents or reports.

Just the other day, as I was approaching the hallway exit at the Janet Goeske center, Delia had always wanted to make things out of clay. So, she said, "let's try this ceramics class. It looks fun and our friend, Joy, is taking it with her husband." Now, I have heard it all. There is definitely no chance of me becoming a couch potato. I do not desire to be one, but one could so easily slide down that path.

I am no longer the overly responsible leader as I was in my job as a mathematician for the Naval Labs in Corona, and later as the chief statistician for the Air Force Audit Agency. Retirement is a significant transformation from my past. I am now happy to pursue whatever dreams appear — reminds me of when I was young and uninhibited.

Vietnam and Me

by Scharlett Stowers Vai

I was totally against the war in Vietnam. What did those people ever do to us? We were invading their homeland. "Why?" I wondered. Why were young men being sent away to die? So many questions and the answers didn't jive. I thought there would be hope if Robert "Bobby" Kennedy became president, but they killed him too. My heart sank lower than it ever had in my lifetime. I was only 14, but I knew the war was wrong.

There were all kinds of rallies against the war — mostly college students. My heart was in it too, so I went to every protest rally believing it would make a difference and our troops would come home. They didn't. So I cried lots of tears, but it didn't change a thing!

I talked to older Vets and they all seemed to agree that we were right to be in Vietnam. Wow! I felt they were sick in the head. They wanted to relive past wars through Vietnam. I thought about it for a long time, which made me feel helpless to do anything.

One day, I heard from my uncle Marcus, who was an MP-Sergeant in WWII. He told me the most important thing to our troops was receiving letters — every day, whenever possible. They were more important than food, sex or anything! Just to know that someone cared and that they were not forgotten.

I started receiving letters from other soldiers — millions of miles away. Through their letters, I was there with them. While reading the letters, I could smell the earth of Vietnam. I could hear the birds and creatures. I could visualize the tall grasses and trees. I could see the beautiful red earth and feel it under my feet.

The soldiers tried not to tell me about the horror that took place there. They didn't need to tell me, I just knew. Somehow I could hear the cries of women and children; the yelling of our troops — both the wounded and able-bodied. "GOD, where are you???" I wondered. I could taste the humidity in the air. But how could

I? Why me??? Am I losing my mind? Could it be my imagination? How could I experience a place I'd never been before?

I began writing to a friend of my sister, Alex Lisby. Boy Alexander Gonzales Lisby was his full birth name — he was about 18 or 19 years old. It made me feel proud to be of use to someone over there. Also, I felt it was my obligation because my sister ignored his letters. I felt a deep hurt that I couldn't explain or tell anyone. Again, I asked myself, "why?" How could my sister be so cold-hearted? It seemed like I was always asking "why?" So I began my letter to Boy/Alex by explaining who I was. I didn't have the heart to tell him about my sister's disinterest.

It was fun in a way. I finally had someone I could talk to; I could speak my mind and my heart freely. I've always been a passionate person. Sometimes, I even shared my tears. (Teardrops were visible on the pages of some of my letters). He was so understanding, so sincere and he actually cared about me and what I had to say. Boy/Alex shared his opinions on various things and always asked me to send him pictures of the latest fashions in clothes and shoes. The latest music, dances, etc. It was so cool going through the newspaper looking for clippings for someone. It really made him happy (I could see his smile). It made me smile too.

I had only met Boy/Alex once and thought he was cute. He had jet black curly hair and brown slanted eyes; beautiful brown skin and straight white teeth. He was about 5 feet, 5 inches tall. But, I knew I would never have a chance to date him because of my young age. Anyway, that was okay; I could still be close to him as a friend.

As time went on, Boy/Alex began to call me "Love" and we began to talk about boys. He warned me to get my education first. He said it would be a waste for me to get tied down with a baby at such a young age. He encouraged me to go to college, which I looked forward to everyday. I worked hard to do that. I even went to summer school and graduated from high school early. I was almost 15 years old.

Boy/Alex sent me a picture of him and a little Vietnamese orphan boy named Tong. He had a sweet loving smile. He was half Vietnamese and half French. But, Tong was unwanted because of his mixed heritage. He was 10 years old and streetwise. But I saw him as a sweet little boy. I wondered what would become of Tong after the war. I still have that picture and look at it from time to time. The same warmth comes over me today — a smile, a deep breath and a sigh.

Some time went by and Boy/Alex decided he wanted to adopt Tong and bring him home, back to the States with him. The only problem was, in those days single-parent adoption was not possible, especially by a single male.

I don't recall which one of us came up with the idea for us to marry. He needed to ask my parent's permission because of my young age. My parents said YES! He had enough respect to ask them. My feet didn't touch the ground for a long time! I still can feel it today. Wow! I'd be MOM, a wife and a woman in a few months! He sent me silk pajamas, (I have everything he sent me), a negligee and a beautiful gold wedding band — a perfect fit — matching his (I still have mine today). I felt the happiest I had ever been in my whole life.

In 1969, he was in Los Angeles, a few hours away. I couldn't wait to see him and Tong, my son! Where was Tong??? Boy/Alex was alone when we met. Tong had written me several letters. What happened to those letters? Now, Boy/Alex was safe with me and my parents.

But where was Tong??? Tong could not be found. The orphanage was bombed, Boy told me. He was so heartbroken and so was I. But, in my heart I knew Tong made it out because he was streetwise. "I bet he is in L.A. with a family of his own," I said. This realization seemed to calm Boy/Alex down and he moved on with his life. Our marriage never happened — he married someone else. They had two little boys. The oldest boy had green eyes like mine. He was supposed to be my son.

Riverside Murals: Visual Storytelling

BY FRANCES J. VÁSQUEZ

You may write me down in history / With your bitter,
twisted lies, / You may trod me in the very dirt / But
still, like dust, I'll rise.

~ Maya Angelou

A renaissance of muralism has emerged in Riverside — like geographic collages, murals are popping up everywhere: alleys, brick walls, behind tall buildings, store fronts, and school buildings. The walls and alleyways of Riverside are adorned with inspirational visual stories: tales, legends and community narratives — portrayed in vibrant images. Mural artists are articulating their voices in art spaces all over town.

Murals impart provocative, illustrative storytelling. Like urban canvasses, murals convey their community's history, values, social justice concerns, and dreams and aspirations of the people. Visual stories have the power to evoke wide-ranging emotions and bring joy and hope and excitement. Many Latino and Black stories chronicle narratives about anger, trauma, racism, and first-hand immigration narratives. Murals are relatable.

There is a visceral connection between visual and literary arts. I pondered, "*Why not merge the inspirations of local murals into literary canvases to put in writing what the muse evokes?*" An inspiration emerged for the spring session of Tesoros de Cuentos, our creative writing group. Applying our art museum docent expertise and incorporating Ekphrastic writing techniques, photographer Kimberly Olvera-Du Bry and I embarked on a mural-hopping adventure.

Tesoros de Cuentos was inspired by a unity event in Riverside in 2016 by then-State Poet Laureate Juan Felipe Herrera. I formed a bilingual, bicultural writing group — Tesoros de Cuentos — with support by the Inlandia Institute. We meet at the SSgt. Salvador J. Lara Casa Blanca Library in the heart of Riverside. We aspire to give literary voice to the Chicana/o community via written stories. We convene workshops to compose and finesse participant's work — culminating in the publication of their best writing in the annual Writing from Inlandia anthology. Informed by the intersection of the rich oral tradition of storytelling and Mexican "Dichos", I created the Tesoros de Cuentos motto: "Las palabras vuelan; los escritos quedan", Spanish for "Words fly; writings endure."

In 2021, we pivoted from initial inward introspection of the memoir to writing memorials about special loved ones. In 2022 Tesoros de Cuentos took an outward and other-directed perspective into the arts community to motivate us to derive writing inspirations from the bountiful murals in Riverside.

Kimberly Olvera-Du Bry and I developed and implemented workshops that took participants on field trips out into the community to view a selection of new murals. Our theme, "Storytelling via the Arts: Riverside Murals," became our mantra for several months.

Like Plein Air artists, our group ventured into the environment to view, discuss and write about the stories and motifs depicted in the murals. Powerful images immerged in reflections of social justice, equity, repression, injustice — also, of love, resilience, triumph, and hope. The images delighted the senses to inspire, elucidate, incite, inform. They also conveyed tales of unity, ancestry, cultural pride and identity. Ah, yes, and love.

Writer and artist Ed Fuentes wrote that "… murals have long been a mechanism for telling the story of place, relating political stances and portraying the heroes of a community." Fuentes affirmed, "Visual tales inhabit a space in mainstream arts culture and a place in the larger narrative of Riverside, adding other storylines." Raised in the Casa Blanca barrio of Riverside, he wrote, "As a kid I looked closely at my street [Fern Street], which at the time lacked sidewalks or curbs, on my two-block walk to the library... At the library, I borrowed books on art, or whatever else I could find to pass the hot summer months, and I noticed there were not many stories about my kind of neighborhood."

An awareness of listening for stories also came while Fuentes watched murals being painted in the neighborhood in the early 1970s by local artists such as Roy Duarte, Jimbo Gutierrez, and others — a direct influence to the art being created in the California farmlands. Many of the murals have since faded, but fragments and shadows remain as evidence of their existence. Fuentes credits Al Kovar, executive director of the Casa Blanca Home of Neighborly Service who "was active in social work and civil rights. He made frequent trips to the Central Valley and saw the start of a mural movement there. Kovar added a community mural project to his busy list and connected local artists to walls in the neighborhood."

Fuentes posits that Chicano-heritage muralism is part of our Chicano DNA —from the long tradition of muralism in México. A compelling new example in Casa Blanca is the César Chávez mural painted by Tony Ray. It celebrates the work and legacy of the United Farm Workers Union and the local residents who shared the struggle for social and environmental justice with Chávez — including Gina Samano, Ginger Anaya, and Rudolfo Rivera who are memorialized in the mural. It can be viewed on Casa Blanca Street.

The "Riverside Tales" mural was painted by a team of local artists led by Pável Acevedo, F.C. Aragon, and Carlos Castro. Guest artists included Maurice Howard, Inland Mujeres, Darren Villegas, among others. It honors the Harada family legacy and names of numerous multicultural Civil Rights luminaries who made local social impact. Acevedo immortalized his then-nine year old daughter Pilar as the goddess Calafia holding her regal staff. On the sunny afternoon of our field trip, former City Councilmember Andy Melendrez greeted us by the mural with a welcome assortment of homemade cookies and agua de Jamaica to refresh us. The imposing mural graces a brick wall in an alley on University Avenue near Orange Street.

Prevalent in numerous Riverside murals is the butterfly motif as a universal symbol of change, hope, and transformation. Mariposa Alley on Ninth Street near City Hall features colorful Monarch butterflies in migration and in various colors and sizes. It was created with repurposed cans by artist and restaurateur Martín Sanchez. Across the alley from the Monarchs is a greeting, "Love Blooms Here." The uplifting "How to Fly" mural was painted by Joey Koslik and Patrick Barwinski. Their fanciful mural features a lovely array of pastel flowers and butterflies.

A side wall at Placita Restaurant features a "Dia de Muertos" mural by Jesus A. Castañeda. The whimsical José Guadalupe Posada-inspired skeletal Mariachis and dancers perform in the foreground of a dark starry night. Much symbolism is depicted in the three panels: Nopal cacti, "papel picado", butterflies, hummingbird, Aztec pyramids, luminous rabbit full moon, and more inspirations. It can be viewed on University Avenue near Chicago Avenue.

Muralist Juan Navarro gave us a tour of the Eastside Arthouse and took us to a mural at nearby El Trigo Restaurant. The splendid mural on the restaurant's side wall was painted mostly by portrait artist Rosana Cortez with Navarro's assistance. It honors the distinctive stitchery of Mexican floral embroidery and the visage of a beautiful Latina adorned with a red rose in her flowing black hair. Sprigs of wheat illuminated by the glow of a full moon frame the mural as if to declare, ¡"Viva la Mujer"! The mural can be seen on Park Avenue.

...The "Riverside Resilience" mural by Darren Villegas adorns the backside of The Box Theater. The impressive mural scales three stories high to tout the city's attributes of arts and innovation: the parent Washington Navel orange tree, its blossoms and fruit; the numerous institutions of higher learning and medicine; support for arts and culture, and local artists. The mural can be viewed on Fairmount Blvd and Mission Inn Avenue. The view from the terrace of Riverside Main Library across Mission Inn Avenue is spectacular.

...Motherly love is boundless. Most mothers would give anything to save a child from harm. One local mother's love inspired the creation of an amazing mosaic mural. Her child had experienced overt racism in school. "She went to school one way and came back a little bit different because of that experience," stated Rochelle Kanatzar in an article by The Inland Voice.

Support came from several artists and friends to create a mural inspired by Maya Angelou's celebrated "Still I Rise" poem: "You may write me down in history / With your bitter, twisted lies, / You may trod me in the very dirt / But still, like dust, I'll rise."

...The "Rise!" mural is located on Market and Ninth Streets. A bench is there to sit and contemplate the 32 unique portraits of notable African Americans who made impacts on American history to show that black is beautiful. We challenged ourselves to identify the names of the portraits depicted in the evocative mosaic.

...The weekly Los Angeles Times "Escapes" e-Newsletter curated by Rachel Schnalzer came to my Email inbox on June 30, 2022 and stated, "Attention, art lovers of Southern California: There's a new museum in town. Earlier this month, The Cheech Marin Center for Chicano Art and Culture of the Riverside Art Museum officially opened its doors to the public. The center is already making history as the only permanent art space to exclusively showcase Chicano and Mexican American art in the country. The newly opened Cheech Marin Center is just one reason to make a beeline to Riverside. There's also a 'renaissance of murals' happening too, according to The Press Enterprise."

"*Wow!*" I thought, "*Someone else used my 'renaissance' reference.*" Quickly, I clicked on the link and became ecstatic when it connected to <u>my</u> Mother's Day story in the Inlandia Literary Journeys column in The Press-Enterprise. Imagine that! A Los Angeles Times journalist appreciated my Riverside's murals story enough to recommend it to their subscribers. Hundreds of thousands of subscribers.... And, to correlate my murals story to The Cheech!

...Art, as depicted in Riverside murals provides an avenue to a diverse range of critical discussions: What is the artist saying to you? How did the images make you feel? What memories did it evoke? Recuerdos...? Images can help us process deep emotions — farm workers in the fields.... They can call us to action as José Guadalupe Posadas did during the Mexican Revolution with his whimsical skeletal characters and iconic Catrina images.

...Readers, I invite you and friends to take a look at the multitude of murals enhancing diverse areas of Riverside — 12th largest city in California. The murals are free to view and parking is usually available nearby. Indeed, visits to The Cheech are indispensable!

...Heartfelt thanks and appreciation to the personnel at SSgt. Salvador J. Lara Casa Blanca Library for providing a comfortable, welcoming meeting place for us to write and read and share our compelling and powerful stories. Sincere thanks and gratitude to the Inlandia Institute for their continued community service sponsorship and publication of our cuentos. ¡Gracias!

Note: An abridged version of this story was published in the Inlandia Literary Journeys Column on Mothers Day, May 12, 2022 in four SCNG newspapers: The Press-Enterprise, The Sun, Inland Valley Daily Bulletin and The Redlands Facts.

Riverside Tales Mural (L-R) Kimberly Olvera Du Bry, Pilar Acevedo, Pável Acevedo, Richard Gonzalez, Bob Garcia, Scharlett Stowers Vai, Frances J. Vásquez, Janine Pourroy Gamblin, Albert Contreras, Andy Melendrez. 3-25-2022. Photo courtesy of Kimberly Olvera Du Bry.

The Big Lie of Christmas

BY JOSE LUIS VIZCARRA

All my life I have been led to believe in Christmas as the most important celebration in our lives. All I heard was that it was important to show how much we loved others by the gifts we wrapped and gave them to countless relatives and friends that supposedly we love. The early decorations in our homes and stores with the seasonal songs created a joyous ambience in the whole Christian world. Most people had to decorate their homes or suffer social criticism from their neighbors and friends. People had to rush to purchase the natural pine trees to place them inside their homes to decorate them with bright lights and spheres. Others decided to decorate with lights the trees and bushes around their properties. The nights became brighter as the day arrived. In my town the posadas are still a popular tradition that the young and the old enjoy. It tells of the troubles that Joseph and Mary had been looking for a place to sleep and maybe give birth to their son, Jesus. It is common to have fire water to fight the cold of the evening as they go from home to home caroling with musical instruments until they reach the designated home to end the search. Then the group hear the most desired words, "It is party time!" There the party starts with delicious traditional dishes and drinks. There was also a required piñata for the youngsters and older people to have fun. The people are always in a party mood at this time of the year leading into the New Year. I loved all the celebrations and excitement of having relatives and friends join us.

Since my early youth I was involved in the spirit of my family and joined in the church services daily, the Posadas, the decorations of the tree and the outside of the house. As several decades have passed I started analyzing the meaning of Christmas. I arrived at the conclusion that it has been a lie instilled into our lives by the churches, the malls, Amazon, and what you should not leave at home. The mob scenes in the malls are a fanatic desperation to not lose the specials or to lose the closest place in the parking lot to the door of the mall. It is pure insanity how millions of dramatic ladies go in droves to the specials on Black Friday leaving the husbands to go to the mall fight after they had the Thanksgiving dinner. Have you ever been crazy to go to the mall and find a parking space? Who said that women are the weak sex? Have you ever been with your lady during the stampede on Black Friday? You would experience a true free for all fighting for the items that are in short supply and both ladies believe that they touched that dress first. It is a true tug-of-war battle. In some cases, the ladies decided to settle it with fingernails and hair pulling. That is why is called a cat fight. The loser is left to hunt for another special on the racks or on the tables. Those big 75% off signs drive the ladies to a frenzy that is only calmed when they carry enough bags that barely fit in their cars that are parked a mile away because the parking lot was full. A few of the ladies were overloaded with the heavy bags that they had to carry wearing high heels that are not proper for manual labor. They wish to have dragged their drunk husbands to help them carry the heavy bags. It is not only the battle with other drivers looking for a spot to park. The long walk from the parking spot to the mall would begin the battle royale to garb the best offers before the other ladies. All the things that a few says later they regret buying. The ladies would not tell the husbands as to how much they spent on the purchases, but only on how much money they had saved.

After much analyzing Christmas I came to the realization that Christmas has been a big lie all my life. Think about the mentality of the people who go all out in debt feeling the social pressure to give presents to everyone regardless as to how much you get into debt just to please many people who only wonder how much the present cost. Human beings are under the delusion that only extremely expensive gifts are worth the friendship. Once you receive one you are now in a situation to reciprocate with another expensive gift too. I believe that giving a gift that you personally made is more valuable emotionally and financially due to the time and effort in creating it with love and care. When I give a gift it is one of the books that I published or one of the anthologies published with the Inlandia Publisher. My first published took me over nine months to create and over $2,500 to bring it to the public. When you purchase one gift, how long did it take you to create that gift? All wise individuals know that time is the most asset that we possess. One day one of my acquaintances confided in me that the season depressed her since she did not have money to buy gifts for her friends. I looked at her and told her, "What are you doing? A true friend does not need a gift to be your friend. If that so called Friend expects a gift that is not cheap, that person is not a friend. Don't be stupid to get into debt just to please anyone. Prepare a meal and write that friend a long letter. That is what a true friend expects. Those are some of the reasons that I believe that Christmas is a very expensive lie.

Why Do I Write?

by Jose Luis Vizcarra

Why do people write?   Why do you write?

Anger and love are my inspiration

All forms of art require them

Immortality is achieved by creating art,

Never compete with the greatest writers of all time

Wasted decades not having a diary to remember my youth
important events

The dullest pencil is sharper than the greatest memory

Practice makes perfect is a lie, perfect practice makes perfect

Ego gets in the way of progress; humility is the greatest aid to
learn

Most of us are ashamed of our lack of grammar and do not
want to be exposed to our deficiencies. It is cured by
reading constantly

People claim that children do not like to write, obviously they
have not seen all the writing on the walls with graffiti

Evidence that the earliest man needed to record their thoughts
on the wall of caves

Once I found my scribe passion I have not been able to stop
after my first published book and five anthologies with the
Inlandia writing groups

Celena, rest in peace, brought the writer in me about three years
ago.

Currently I am working on close to 30 novels and over 100
poems in English and Spanish

I have written one non-fiction book about my experiences in
education, business, and investments

Seeing your book published it takes as long as to have a child,
nine months

Anyone can write a book,

The only requirement is to be able to tell a story

You do not have to publish it

The greatest art that was never created is in the mind of the
cadaver in the cemetery

You do not have to write it. You can record your voice, paint,
sculpt or be a mime

I follow these steps

Idea

Write it before the idea leaves me

Begin the story

Create interesting characters with my idea what a man and a
woman make them strong

Come up with the most difficult problems

The characters are wise to overcome the adversity

I include wisdom that I have learned from the best literature to
pass it onto the reader to make them think

It Goes Around

by Ilyn Welch

Tony can't bring himself to leave the house.

The auto-shop owner became a paranoid, haunted germaphobe after Pavel the recluse died. Though his own heart teeters on failure, Tony is terrified of anesthetized surgery. Insomnia keeps him miserable.

Pavel was the last of four deaths connected to Tony. He passed in a nearby century-old house, built by his circus-performer ancestors, a chest of gold allegedly hidden in its foundation. Self-confined for decades, Pavel depended on Tony for meals and necessities. Tony also paid the property taxes, therefore becoming the owner after Pavel died, a method he used to acquire other houses in the old neighborhood. Tony invested in a deep-seeking metal detector, sweeping the premises for a short period.

The three other men who died, on separate occasions, were all crackerjack auto mechanics on the skids. Each had a turn living in a camper shell in Tony's car-part-strewn yard, in exchange for free labor in his repair garage. The first two overdosed in the camper barely a couple months apart. Stevie, the last one found stiff in the camper, was second cousin to Pavel, an alcoholic, and the best mechanic of them all.

Now Tony lives in the tormented shell of his own body, unable to dig for his gold.

Contributor Bios

Janet Lako Alexander is a poet, writer, and bilingual educator. A UC Riverside graduate, she was born in Blythe and raised in Rubidoux, California. Her works have appeared in Writing from Inlandia and other publications. She teaches poetry writing/performance for the Ontario-Montclair School District, where she has facilitated the district's annual Poetry Celebration.

Margit Andersson was born in northern Sweden. She has lived in Hemet for several years and enjoys taking part in the Joy Writers group in Redlands every week.

Don Bennet has worn many hats during his life: Deputy DA, private practice lawyer, food bank director, consultant, trainer, husband, father, grandpa, and heart transplant recipient. He found out about the Redlands Joslyn Joy Writers after reading a newspaper article about them, and joined their Zoom group in the summer of 2020.

Karen Bradford, M.A. is an award-winning writer and photographer and an elected board of education trustee. She was the public relations manager for The Press-Enterprise and a campus communications officer at the University of California, Riverside. She has written two collections of local nonfiction history.

Mary Briggs is a 1'st generation, Mexican American, born in 1939, to a family of migrant workers, raised in EastLos Angeles, has resided in Riverside since 1991.

Stephanie A. Bruce was born in Devore California where she still lives in her family home. She was a singer and dance instructor for most of her life. She is a retired personal caregiver. Stephanie says she wishes she had discovered her passion for writing a long time ago. [Joslyn Joy Writers with Mae Wagner Marinello]

Walking amongst Riverside trees inspires **Georgette Geppert Buckley's** paintings. The LMU Alumna glides through meditative Tai Chi Chih, or writes procedural aftermaths and fantastical visions, prompted by Wil Clarke's Celena's Scribes. Georgette concocts delectable gluten and dairy free sustenance. She and her husband celebrated their 41st anniversary in San Diego.

Lesslie Alvarez Burhans is the CFO of her company specializing in Trade Compliance. She holds a Finance Degree from Baruch College and an MBA from the University of Connecticut. Lesslie was brought to the United States at the age of four from Mexico City and grew up in Brooklyn, New York.

Alben Chamberlain is a native of the Inland Empire. He graduated with an AA from San Bernardino Valley College. He received a BA Degree from BYU-Hawaii and an MBA from the American Graduate School. He has served as a supply officer in the US Navy Reserve, a federal bank auditor, a teacher in local high schools and middle schools, as well as a retirement counselor with a major insurance company. He has a wife and three grown children.

Natalie Champion participated in the Chronologyland workshop. She is a poet and kindergarten teacher. She is from the Inland Empire, but lives in San Francisco with her husband Rick and cat Milo Morris.

Rick Champion is a writer, photographer, and mathematician.

This past year **Sylvia Clarke** participated in two Inlandia Writing Workshops. The first, Rose Y. Monge's Writing Warriors class, focused on memoir, and the second, Celena's Scribes led by Wil Clarke, gave room for sharing writing in any genre. Both encouraged her creative writing endeavors.

Wil Clarke, after a long career of teaching college mathematics on two continents, enjoys the freedom of writing. He especially enjoys appreciating others' creations as they brandish their skills through Celena's Scribes Inlandia Writers' Workshop.

James Coats is a poet, performer, and educator born in Los Angeles and raised in the Inland Empire. With a passion for all things creative, he strives to capture authentic self-expression through his imagistic narrative poetry. You can find him attending poetry readings throughout California or follow him on Instagram @ MrLovingWords.

Elinor Cohen wanted to be an astronomer but couldn't commit to all the math. So instead she got a degree in Pre-Modern Literature that she never uses. Elinor resides with family in the desolate desert after decades as an Angeleno, and is fully obsessed with her rescue dog Floof.

Albert Contreras resides in Fontana with his daughter and son-in-law. He is proud of his role of raising eight children — beginning at the age of 19. He enjoys writing, especially poetry.

Carlos Cortés is the Edward A. Dickson Emeritus Professor of History and co-director of the School of Medicine's Health Equity, Social Justice, and Anti-Racism curriculum at the University of California, Riverside. He is the Consulting Humanist for The Cheech and the Creative/Cultural Advisor for Nickelodeon's "Dora the Explorer" and "Go, Diego, Go!"

Cait Danielle is a poet from the Inland Empire. When not working, Cait spends time holding open mics, studying astrology, and hanging out with friends. Cait received a BA in Creative Writing from CSU Long Beach and will be attending UC Riverside for graduate school.

Chuck Doolittle has enjoyed writing his whole life. His teachers supported him, he continued on to teach it, and he's now enjoying this creative style with other seniors in his area. He hopes you appreciate his writing style and that it might encourage you to pick up a pen.

Reiss DuPlessis was born in New Orleans, Louisiana but has resided in California all of his adult life. His career was as a civil servant with the State of California after stints in the worlds of retail books, publishing and a short career as a folk singer. He loves all genres of music with classical and operatic at the top of his list. He is an avid reader who carries his iPad at all times in order to read the latest downloaded book whenever there is a free minute.

His addiction to reading can be traced to his early childhood. He was told by his family that if nothing else was available, when he was a preschooler, he would read the cereal box. After many years of bureaucratic writing, he has decided to try writing for pleasure.

Jerry Ellingson lives in Redlands, California. Her goal is to record family stories so her genealogy work will not only have photos and statistics, but stories that should be told. She is a retired teacher with a Bachelor's degree in Dance and English. Her Master's degree is in education. The greatest joys in her life have been teaching Graphic Design and Computer to adults and her role as a mother and grandmother. [Joslyn Joy Writers with Mae Wagner Marinello]

Ellen Estilai's poetry and prose have appeared in several journals and anthologies, including *Alimentum; Snapdragon: A Journal of Art and Healing; Ink & Letters; Heron Tree; (In)Visible Memoirs, Vol. 2.; Writing from Inlandia; SHARK REEF;* and *Lady Liberty Lit.* Her memoir, *Exit Prohibited*, will be published by Inlandia Books in 2023.

Nan Friedley is a retired special education teacher and graduate of Ball State University, Muncie, IN. Her writings have been published in a poetry chapbook, *Short Bus Ride* by *Bad Knee Press, Indiana Voice Journal, Inlandia Anthologies* and *Three*, a nonfictional anthology collection by Push Pen Press. Nan participates in a variety of Inlandia workshops.

Fred García (he/they) is a Xicanx writer and creative writing student at UC Riverside. His work explores inherited cycles of existence and poetry as medicine.

Ragini Goel has a master's degree in Sanskrit and a teacher's degree in English. People who know Ragini describe her as a Renaissance woman with varied interests. Ragini is an appointed commissioner to the Human Relations Council. Ragini says her best achievements are her two sons Sumeet and Amit.

Mark Grinyer has published poems in *Rattle, The Literary Review, The Spoon River Quarterly, The Pacific Review, Perigee,* and elsewhere. In 2017, he published a chapbook: *Approaching Poetry.* He was educated at the University of California, Riverside, where he began publishing poetry, and received a PhD in English and American Literature. He now lives on the edge of the Cleveland National Forest in Southern California.

Carmen Melendez-Gutierrez was born in Comerio, Puerto Rico on July 25, 1954. She currently resides in Riverside, California. Graduated from San Diego State University. She worked for the United States Postal Service. She is also a Life Coach. Her major achievement is the publishing of her book titled *Yuya's Adventures.*

Milan Hamilton, resident of Redlands, California since 1979, has been writing for many years. As a pastor and college teacher he wrote scholarly papers and lectures, as well as sermons. As a non-profit executive, he wrote fundraising letters. As a retired person he began memoir writing, joined a writers group at the beginning of the century. He published a blog for several years and has since concentrated on poetry. He is a member of the Academy of American Poets.

Edna Heled is an artist, art therapist, counsellor and travel journalist from NZ. She studied Art Therapy (MA) overseas and Psychology (Hons) at the University of Auckland. Her writing includes short stories, poetry, travel writing and non-fiction. She has been published in many anthologies in NZ, Australia, USA, and more.

Richard Hess is a retired physician. He practiced Obstetrics/Gynecology in Fairbanks, Alaska for 41 years. He is now living in Springdale, Arkansas with his wife, Marie. He enjoys writing about his medical and other life experiences.

Connie Jameson, retired elementary and special education teacher, enjoys writing children's picture books, poetry and short stories. Connie also enjoys reading, travel, nature, antiques, theater and

Toastmasters. Her first published book is *Dating 'n' Mating: Wit and Wisdom on Love and Marriage*.

Ann Kanter grew up in Riverside and is semi-retired, practicing immigration law in Sacramento. She enjoys her connection with writers from Inlandia's Adventures in Chronology class. Her bilingual poems have been published in *Voices of the New Sun* (Atzlan Cultural 2004) and *We Came to Dream* (CantoHondo 2016).

Margo Klein is a retired CPA who recently moved to Redlands after her home was damaged in Hurricane Ian.

Joan Koerper (Dr. Mary Joan Koerper), has lived in the Inland Empire for over 36 years, residing in Redlands, Riverside and, for the last nine years in Wrightwood. Published in all genres, she had been part of the Inlandia Institute since the beginning of the effort.

Jessica Lea's poetry, photos, and artwork have appeared in *Spectrum Magazine, Inlandia, Writer's on the Block zine, A Visual God* (2022 Elyssar Press), and *United Church of Christ Living Psalms*. She was part of Riverside Art Museum's 52 Project 2019 and 2021 Exhibitions, and authored Diamonds and Yoga Pants (2020).

Robin Woodruff Longfield was born in Atlanta, GA, but moved to Southern California at an early age. She has been an Inland Empire resident for many years. Her work has appeared in several literary journals and anthologies. She still believes in Magic and possibilities.

Mae Wagner Marinello has been a part of Inlandia since 2008. She began facilitating a weekly workshop at the Joslyn Senior Center in Redlands in 2014. When the pandemic hit, the Joslyn Joy Writers never missed a beat, meeting weekly via Zoom. They continue as a hybrid group with some writers attending in person and some attending via Zoom from as far away as Ireland and Arkansas. Mae is a mother of three, grandmother of nine and great-grandmother of seven. She lives in Redlands with her joyful little dog named Cricket.

Terry Lee Marzell lives in Chino Hills, California. Now retired, she taught school for 36 years. She earned her BA in English from CSUF, her MA in Interdisciplinary Studies from CSUSB, and a Library Science credential from CSULB. Terry has published two books, *Chalkboard Champions* (2012) and *Chalkboard Heroes* (2015).

Phyllis Maynard has enjoyed So. Calif. for most of her life. She is currently a member of the Writing Warriors (Memoirs Anthology) group. The treasure of her retirement years has been the time and opportunity to write, where her style tap dances from humor to heartache.

Mary McLoughlin born in Amityville, N.Y. Graduated in 1969 from Bethpage high school then took off to Ireland, met Frank in his brother's pub in Dundalk. In 1988 brought family to the U.S ending in Redlands. Found Joslyn Joywriters in 2014.

Rose Y. Monge has facilitated the memoir class at the Goeske Center since 2009. She believes writing a memoir is powerful: healing and therapeutic for the writer and inspirational and educational for the reader. She's a Mexican immigrant who honors her parents' legacy of life lessons in her memoir. Advocating social justice, diversity and inclusion are her passions.

An active senior, **Barbara Mortenson** is retired from a career in international corporate management and a second career as an adjudicator for the State of California. She has served on many charity boards and is an activist for women's and other civil rights. Her love of music led her to be the driving force in bringing the Metropolitan Opera live simulcasts to the greater Palms Springs/Coachella Valley area. She is a published writer of memoir and incidental biographical essays. Barbara is a foodie and has met few meals she didn't like. She lives with her husband and a houseful of rescue dogs and cats.

Jane O'Shields-Hayner is a writer and visual artist living in Southern California. Jane writes non-fiction, fiction and poetry and publishes in *Tiferet Journal, Friends Journal, HerStry* and elsewhere. With a biophilic compassion for the natural world and an unflinching look at life's poignant absurdities, Jane provokes our laughter and leaves us with lingering questions.

Bonnie Parmenter is a retired teacher, curious and tenacious. In her ninth decade, she has decided to participate in the heady joy of writing in Victoria Waddles' workshop and in Wil Clarke's. She lives in Moreno Valley with her husband and four cats.

Christine Petzar lives in Riverside and participated in her first writers' workshop in 2019. Her career in educational administration involved professional writing and teacher education related to English Learners. In retirement, she is branching out to more personal writing—memoir and creative non-fiction.

Writing creatively through Inlandia Institute has brought **Cindi Pringle** full circle to youthful endeavors prior to her nearly 40-year career in journalism and corporate communication. Since 2018 she has focused on poetry and fiction; in fall 2022 she joined the Writing for Children workshop and is developing several projects.

Janet Rendall has won several fiction writing awards from the Santa Barbara Writers Conference. She published her debut novel, *Route 66 to the Milky Way*, in 2015 and a stand-a-lone sequel, *TubeLight*, in 2017. She is published in several scientific journals and in hand rehabilitation textbooks.

Kate Feinberg Robins lives in Redlands with her partner and son. She teaches Pilates, fitness, and adult ballet through her online business Find Your Center Arts and Wellness. She is a linguistic anthropologist and a former principal dancer with the Cuyahoga Valley Youth Ballet.

Leslie Roundy is a long-time resident of Redlands, California and began writing with Joslyn Joy Writers in 2022. She utilized her writing skills throughout her career in marketing and human resources. Now that she is retired, Leslie is pursuing her passion for writing more creatively. She also enjoys watercolor painting and gardening.

Patricia L. Scruggs is a retired art educator. In addition to her poetry collection, Forget the Moon, her work has appeared in *ON-THEBUS*, *Spillway*, *Rip Rap*, *Cultural Weekly*, *Crab Creek Review*, *Burningwood*, *MacQueen's Quinterly*, as well as the anthologies *13 Los Angeles Poets*, *So Luminous the Wildflowers*, and *Beyond the Lyric Moment*.

Kristine Ann Shell lives in Redlands, California, where she participates in the Joslyn Writers Group and the Inlandia Institute. Kristine is a retired school administrator and teacher. She holds Bachelor of Arts degrees in English and Secondary Education. She also holds Master of Education degrees in Elementary Reading and School Administration. Kristine has been with the Inlandia Institute since October, 2016.

Carolyn L. Snow has been writing short stories and poetry for many years. She is an elementary school teacher and she enjoys riding her bike, going to the beach, and spending time with friends and family members.

David Stone teaches English at Loma Linda Academy. His poetry has been published in *New Verse News*, *Identity Theory*, and *Shuf*. He's been a guest writer for the Press Enterprise's Inlandia Literary Journeys columns for nine years. He is a former poetry editor for Inlandia: A Literary Journey.

Heather Takenaga (her/she) is a writer and poet. Born and raised in Riverside, CA. Currently writing short stories and poetry. Drooling for cat cuddles, bedtime snuggles, and a reading vacation.

Elizabeth Uter is an award-winning poet winning the 2018 Poem for Slough Competition. She's facilitated poetry workshops; performed at festivals. She is published in: *Writings from Inlandia*, *Poetry anthologies: Welcome To Britain; Bollocks To Brexit; BeWILDering Poems; Gitanjali and Beyond, Womanhood; Echoes, Vol. 2; This Is Our Place - A Nature Anthology*.

Gudelia Vaden (Delia), is a teacher, poet, writer and artist. Her writings reflect the importance of family. She illustrates and contributes to Natalie's Zine, an on-line magazine. While teaching, she received a BA degree from California State University, San Bernardino. Her stories can be found in "Writing from Inlandia" publications.

Thomas Vaden earned a MS degree in Mathematics from the University of Missouri Columbia. Originally from St. Louis, Tom enlisted in the Air Force and married Gudelia at Castle AFB in the San Joaquin Valley. He is a writer, poet and enjoys art, math, and hands-on hobbies.

Scharlett Stowers Vai is a lifelong resident of the Casa Blanca Barrio for 71 years. She is totally bilingual — reads and writes Spanish. She is a Brown Beret and activist for la Causa, even though she is racially mixed. She is a supporter of Inlandia.

Frances J. Vásquez is Director Emerita of Inlandia Institute and is passionate about Chicana/o history and culture, Celebrating Cultura and Tesoros de Cuentos. She graduated from Riverside schools: Poly, RCC, and UCR, where she earned AA, BS and MBA Degrees. Frances facilitates Tesoros de Cuentos Creative Writing Workshops in Riverside.

Jose Luis Vizcarra has been involved with Inlandia for several wonderful years of learning the power of the written word. The inspiration was a great instructor, Celena RIP, who opened the floodgates of creating poetry and novels. He discovered the two keys to write: PASSION AND MOTIVATION. Seeing his first published novel, *Kiss from an Angel* gave him immortality by leaving a legacy.

Ilyn Welch (she/her) writes horror, mystery and creative nonfiction from the Inland Empire in Southern California. Her work has been published with *PANK,* Shotgun Honey, *Pomona Valley Review,* and Bag of Bones Press.

About Inlandia Institute

Inlandia Institute is a regional literary non-profit and publishing house. We seek to bring focus to the richness of the literary enterprise that has existed in this region for ages. The mission of the Inlandia Institute is to recognize, support, and expand literary activity in all of its forms in Inland Southern California by publishing books and sponsoring programs that deepen people's awareness, understanding, and appreciation of this unique, complex and creatively vibrant region.

The Institute publishes books, presents free public literary and cultural programming, provides in-school and after school enrichment programs for children and youth, holds free creative writing workshops for teens and adults, and boot camp intensives. In addition, every two years, the Inlandia Institute appoints a distinguished jury panel from outside of the region to name an Inlandia Literary Laureate who serves as an ambassador for the Inlandia Institute, promoting literature, creative literacy, and community. Laureates to date include Susan Straight (2010-2012), Gayle Brandeis (2012-2014), Juan Delgado (2014-2016), Nikia Chaney (2016-2018), and Rachelle Cruz (2018-2020).

To learn more about the Inlandia Institute, please visit our website at www.InlandiaInstitute.org.

Inlandia Books

Writing from Inlandia, an annual anthology

Breaking Pattern by Tisha Marie Reichle-Aguilera

Exit Prohibited by Ellen Estilai

These Black Bodies Are…, edited by Romaine Washington

Pretend Plumber by Stephanie Barbé Hammer

Ladybug by Nikia Chaney

Vital: The Future of Healthcare, edited by RM Ambrose

Güero-Güero: The White Mexican and Other Published and Unpublished Stories by Dr. Eliud Martínez

A Short Guide to Finding Your First Home in the United States: An Inlandia anthology on the immigrant experience

Care: Stories by Christopher Records

San Bernardino, Singing, edited by Nikia Chaney

Facing Fire: Art, Wildfire, and the End of Nature in the New West by Douglas McCulloh

In the Sunshine of Neglect: Defining Photographs and Radical Experiments in Inland Southern California,1950 to the Present by Douglas McCulloh

Henry L. A. Jekel: Architect of Eastern Skyscrapers and the California Style by Dr. Vincent Moses and Catherine Whitmore

Orangelandia: The Literature of Inland Citrus edited by Gayle Brandeis

While We're Here We Should Sing by The Why Nots

Go to the Living by Micah Chatterton

No Easy Way: Integrating Riverside Schools – A Victory for Community by Arthur L. Littleworth

Hillary Gravendyk Prize
poetry series

How to Know You're Dreaming When You're Dreaming by
Angelica Maria Barraza Tran
Winner of the 2021 National Hillary Gravendyk Prize

Our Lady of Perpetual Desert by Alexandra Martinez
Winner of the 2021 Regional Hillary Gravendyk Prize

among the enemies by Michael Samra
Winner of the 2020 National Hillary Gravendyk Prize

This Side of the Fire by Jonathan Maule
Winner of the 2020 Regional Hillary Gravendyk Prize

The Silk the Moths Ignore by Bronwen Tate
Winner of the 2019 National Hillary Gravendyk Prize

Remyth: A Postmodernist Ritual by Adam Martinez
Winner of the 2019 Regional Hillary Gravendyk Prize

Former Possessions of the Spanish Empire by Michelle Peñaloza
Winner of the 2018 National Hillary Gravendyk Prize

All the Emergency-Type Structures by Elizabeth Cantwell
Winner of the 2018 Regional Hillary Gravendyk Prize

Our Bruises Kept Singing Purple by Malcolm Friend
Winner of the 2017 National Hillary Gravendyk Prize

Traces of a Fifth Column by Marco Maisto
Winner of the 2016 National Hillary Gravendyk Prize

God's Will for Monsters by Rachelle Cruz
Winner of the 2016 Regional Hillary Gravendyk Prize
Winner of the 2018 American Book Award

Map of an Onion by Kenji C. Liu
Winner of the 2015 National Hillary Gravendyk Prize

All Things Lose Thousands of Times by Angela Peñaredondo
Winner of the 2015 Regional Hillary Gravendyk Prize

www.ingramcontent.com/pod-product-compliance
Lightning Source LLC
Chambersburg PA
CBHW070445030726
47503CB00004B/902